A Forgotten Door Called Home

A Forgotten Door Called Home

Rev. Cheryl Anne Kincaid

To Christian women everywhere who are looking for a sense of home.

Table of Contents

†

Chapter One

Pastor Mike's Journey: Joy and Despair for Karrie.

Pastor Mike smiled as Karrie descended from the pulpit. Her face glowed as her mother's arms enveloped her. Pride over Karrie's triumph swelled up inside of him because of Karrie's testimony that she worried about for weeks. But she had succeeded. She had spoken the truth that had burned inside her soul for the last ten years. When Pastor Mike first met her, she could barely whisper about her abuse and journey through foster care. Now she had shared it with the entire congregation and as she stood unashamed as described God's presence during her journey to empowerment from abuse. He watched a wave of relief ripple through her.

He watched her as she disappeared into a crowd of her friends. Josh, Tom, and their parents surrounded her and her mother with hugs and gave much-needed accolades for her courage.

He watched from the back of the sanctuary, feeling Karrie's triumph, and rejoicing in the tiny miracle that had emerged from the horrible drama that had helplessly watched in Karrie's life over the past three years. As he pushed his way through the crowd to congratulate his young disciple, he felt a tug on his sleeve.

"Remember, hon." Rebeca looked into Mike's eyes, "We're having the Whitneys over tonight after church."

"The Whitneys?" he stammered.

He looked down at his wife, Rebecca. At only five feet tall, she was a powerhouse. Her red curly hair and freckled nose made her look childishly cute, but an iron fist lay under Rebecca's velvet glove. With a glow of domestic bliss, she made sure every bill was paid and every social obligation met. As a lawyer in the courtroom, she was a merciless opponent, squeezing every bit of truth from a witness with her quick, intricately pointed questions.

They had met in college. Although a year younger than Mike, Rebecca was already studying law in graduate school while he was still a junior in philosophy. An overachiever, Rebeca easily sailed through college in three years while on campus. Christian clubs kept drawing Mike away from education. But they both caught the ministry bug on a missionary trip to Mexico they had taken with a large college church group. When Mike informed her that he wanted to be a Pastor, she knew she would be the primary breadwinner if their relationship turned serious. She didn't mind because she loved Mike, Christ, and the gospel. But after fifteen years of youth ministry, holding her career and home together wore on her.

"Yes, Mike, the Whitneys. From seminary. You remember." Rebecca's piercing blue eyes searched his face.

Mike closed his eyes. "Oh, yeah. The Whitneys. Sorry. I forgot for a moment."

"It's okay," Rebecca said. "I just want you to be one hundred percent with us this evening."

"Of course, but we agreed that for me to be one hundred percent with you in the evening, I must be fully present where I am right now and I really want to talk to Karrie before she leaves, so this conversation is going to have to wait."

"Yes," Rebecca said as if deliberating a jury settlement. Then she squeezed Mike's hand and looked playfully into his eyes. "Karrie spoke beautifully today. You did a good job, babe." She stood on tip toes and gave him a soft peck on his lips.

Mike squeezed her hand to give a quiet "goodbye for now" and tried to step into the crowd to find Karrie when Anthony White, a church elder, blocked his way.

"Pastor Mike," Anthony said. "I'm sorry to tell you this, but the personnel committee wants to meet with you about Friday night's incident."

"You mean with Lo'laini's father? You realize he's dead, don't you?" Mike's forehead wrinkled. "He left behind a teenage girl with no immediate family to take care of her."

"I've heard something to that effect, but—"

"And shouldn't that be our main concern?" interrupted Pastor Mike.

"I agree with you, but you realize Mike, I'm not just speaking for myself. I'm speaking for the committee."

"Of course," Pastor Mike sighed. "When does the committee want to meet?"

"We know you have the funeral this week, so maybe next week. Tuesday at four thirty?"

Pastor Mike nodded warily.

Anthony's voice softened. "I'm sorry, Mike. I think you did a great job with Karrie and Lo'laini, and if it were up to me, I would say, who cares about a chip off the church patio? We're here to save souls. But it's not only up to me. You understand, don't you?"

"Yeah, I understand." Pastor Mike rubbed his eyes and slapped Anthony on the back. When he looked up, Karrie was gone.

He made his way through the smiles to the parking lot, where he spied Karrie and her mother in their car. He started walking toward them when he heard Karrie's mother scream.

"You idiot! You don't think, girl, do you?" Soda trickled down the side of the car.

The rage and hatred in her voice caught Pastor Mike off guard. Karrie's action certainly wasn't deserving of her mother's response. Karrie made a sarcastic joke, but her face flushed when she saw him staring at her. He hesitated, then turned to another person to make small talk while inwardly berating himself for his cowardice.

After Church, Mike and Rebecca met up with their old seminary friends. Under Rebecca's sharp eye, he tried to stay engaged while they reminisced about their graduate school foibles, but his mind kept returning to the church parking lot. His cowardly reaction haunted him throughout the rest of the night.

***

Monday morning, Mike sat in a clergy meeting in the back of a coffee shop, musing over the week's event. He had been excited about the meeting, which promised an opportunity for the local churches to unite to proclaim Christ, but he couldn't focus. The speaker's words blurred together in a monotone of *blah, blah, blah.*

Questions and regrets clouded his mind. He should have stopped Daniel and Lo'laini from getting in that car. *I should've grabbed the keys from Lo'laini's father.* No, then Daniel would have started throwing punches and that would have been a pretty site for the congregation. For a moment, Mike thought he heard his old Sunday school teacher's voice echo in his head, "What would Jesus do?"

He smiled and shook his head. "I wish I knew," he mumbled.

Three months earlier, Daniel started attending the men's Bible study. He said he wanted to turn his life around. Mike remembered with pride when Daniel brought his drug paraphernalia to church to throw it away because he said he was over that nightmare. Pastor Mike praised God when Daniel testified to throwing it away. Mike thought God had finally answered Lo'laini's prayers. Wednesday night's spectacle proved that he hadn't.

Blah, blah, blah, the speaker's voice droned on. Doubts and questions continued to swirl in Pastor Mike's head. In a matter of seconds, Karrie went from being greatly admired to being deeply shamed by her mother. How had Karrie's victory so quickly turned into defeat? After being in heaven on Sunday morning, what kind of hell was she going to wake up in on

Monday morning? *Blah, blah, blah.* The meeting closed in prayer, and Mike started to get up when another pastor approached him. He was a tall, eloquently dressed black man.

"Pastor Mike?" he said with a deep resounding voice as he extended his hand.

"Yes, you were at the service yesterday."

"I was. I'm Pastor Will Leister, Karrie's old pastor." He pulled up a chair and sat next to Pastor Mike.

"She speaks well of you."

"That was quite a victory for that girl yesterday."

"I thought so too, but now I'm not so sure." Pastor Mike rubbed his eyes. "I wanted to congratulate Karrie after her talk, but she'd already left. I followed her to the parking lot and saw her mother lay into her for a minor infraction. Her voice was full of hatred and anger. It was underserved, and it hurt me to see how Karrie laughed it off, making light of the offense." He heaved a sigh as he stirred his coffee.

He took a long drink of his coffee. "After a week like this last one, I wonder if I'm doing any good or if I hinder the cause of Christ more than I help it."

"Before you condemn yourself, it might help to have some background on that family," Pastor Will said as he sized up the young pastor in front of him. "I felt the same way when I tried to help Karrie's mom. I remember when Moriah first came to our church with her pretty face discolored with brown and red bruises. We all knew something bad was going on at home. People were friendly to her, but no one really knew what to do. She got involved in a small group Bible study. I think everyone was relieved when her husband went back to prison. Then her baby bump began to grow. She already had two older unkempt boys. I couldn't blame her. She hardly knew how to take care of herself, much less her children. I wondered how she was going to make it. Then I thought I saw the victory that would change everything. She came forward after a sermon I preached on Job's recovery. I said that the Bible listed his daughter's name to represent that his wealth and blessings had returned. I said he named his second daughter Keziah, which was a type of incense they burned in prayer. That part of the story spoke to Moriah. During that sermon, she believed that God had spoken to her, that he had answered her prayers. In retrospect, I think that with her husband gone, she started to feel a little more prosperous. She seemed to have a real conversion. She took out a mortgage on her house and bought the beauty parlor where she'd been working. She even named the little girl she was carrying Karrie after Job's third daughter.

"Then her husband came home and said he had accepted Christ in jail. I had fears about the situation. I wanted to tell her to leave him because I was frightened that he would hurt those kids. But I also wanted to believe in his conversion. I believe Jesus can change lives."

Pastor Will heaved a sigh. "My greatest regret is that I encouraged her to stay with him and that…" He blinked away a tear. "That was when Karrie's dad violated her. His conversion had seemed real enough. When he got out of jail, he came to men's Bible study and to church. I guess he…"

"He loved his addictions more?" Mike asked. "The same was true with Lo'laini's dad. He had a conversion too."

"Wasn't that Karrie's best friend? I've heard about her."

Pastor Mike nodded. "I remember when Lo'laini first came to church. We have a ministry that reaches out to foster kids. I was glad to see how well she fit in. But for such a little girl, she seemed alone, and that gave me pause. She was independent and feisty, but she had a hard shell built around her. I wondered what had happened to her to make her build such a barrier and what that barrier was doing to her. But she seemed to be growing in her faith. Then she brought Karrie to church, and Karrie had no shell whatsoever to protect her. It was great to see their faith grow. Even their little romances with two of the boys in our group were endearing to watch. But their pain was always there. It was visible, no matter how hard they tried to hide it. When Karrie started to talk about her faith with confidence, I thought some healing had finally happened in that family."

"Were you thinking this one victory in Karrie's life was going to change her world?" Pastor Will asked, looking directly into Pastor Mike's eyes. "I made the same mistake with Moriah. One prayer may reunite us with God, but sadly, it doesn't erase all the obstacles we're born with."

Pastor Mike shook his head. "I thought I felt a calm assurance that things were going to change for Karrie."

"And so, they have." Pastor Will nodded. "And they will continue to change, but if you heard a voice that said God would rescue her from all trials, I'd ignore that voice. It wasn't from my God because my God doesn't lie. And that vision, son, is a lie. You know the Bible as well as I do, including all the prophets and the apostles whose personal flaws and obstacles haunted them. We all know about the apostle Paul's thorn. Although Paul doesn't specify what kind of thorn it was, most of us can speculate. Karrie's been hurt a lot, and I don't think her thorns will be easily overcome, but she'll get there. Give her time. She'll get there."

Pastor Mike nodded. "I wanted to make her life better. Isn't that what faith is supposed to do?"

"You could say that if Christianity were a soda pop commercial." Pastor Will leaned back in his chair. "You know, there is something seriously wrong with this bubble-gum theology that teaches us that God is simply here to make our fondest wishes come true. The gospel gives us salvation from our sins, but it doesn't mean we still don't suffer the consequences of sin after we've been saved. The cruel consequences of sin have injured many an innocent soul. Sometimes we can't stop that. It's our job to proclaim Christ's salvation. We don't have power over the message after it leaves our mouths. What people do with our messages is between them and God, but I think God is going to work something out in those two girls' lives that neither of us can imagine. I remember reading somewhere that we pastors have this hope that the power is of God and not of us."

Pastor Mike smiled. "You read that book too?"

"I wish I could've spared Karrie that humiliation in the church parking lot. But most of all, I wish I could have stopped Dan from destroying his life and Lo'laini's. I hated witnessing Lo'laini lose her father."

"Sounds like Lo'laini's been losing her father for a long time now." Pastor Will took a long sip of his coffee, "if her family is as complicated as Karrie's. I think both those girls have a lot harder times ahead of them."

They were both silent as they looked into their coffee cups.

"Take me seriously here, young man," Pastor Will said, leaning in. "You gave both those girls a great gift. You gave them each a Christian identity and a Christian fellowship that gave them refuge during their storms. In the end, that is the gift that will get them through all the trials they are going to have to face because no one goes through what they have gone through without the consequences of other people's bad decisions. They've got obstacles and wounds that may get in the way of finding happiness right away, but I think that they will find it."

"And in regard to that incident, you witnessed in the parking lot with Karrie? I've witnessed similar incidents. No matter how good her fortune may be, she will always have to overcome her mother's criticisms and her father's abuse. Add to that her brother's normalizing the crimes committed against her, and you've got some serious obstacles. Don't let those obstacles cause you to undermine the gift you've given her. You gave her permission to use her voice and the ability to see her tragedies in the light of the gospel of Jesus Christ. That gift is going to help her climb out of any dark hole she finds herself in, whether she digs it or someone else pushes her in."

"I don't know. I guess I'm just tired," mumbled Pastor Mike.

"I get it. It's been a tough week for you. When I heard about Daniel's death and the spectacle that played out on your church's front steps, I started to pray for you, young man."

"Who hasn't heard about it? I'm surprised it hasn't been on the news." Pastor Mike handed Will a letter from the personnel committee.

"So, they're flexing their muscles, are they?" Pastor Will smiled as he read the letter. "Most parishioners don't know what we do or why we do it, do they?" He shook his head in disbelief. "Yeah, they're deeply concerned about the situation. What are you going to tell them at this meeting?"

"I am going to tell them I was doing my job." Mike lifted his head.

"You'd be right in telling them that," Will said. "This committee saw a 'reckless situation' Friday night. You know what I saw Sunday morning? I saw a frightened disciple walk on stormy waters because you called her out of the boat."

Mike smiled as Will nodded.

"While you're in with that committee, remind them why a church building exists. And get yourself a vacation. You look worn, son. Was that little redhead sitting next to you Sunday, your wife?"

"Yep, a woman whose love and devotion I feel unworthy of."

"You take her out of town and remind her why she fell in love with a Pastor in the first place." Pastor Will smiled. "Yes, sir. I saw Karrie walk on water Sunday, and I am awfully glad that you beckoned her out of that boat."

✝

Chapter Two

The Storms in Lo'laini's Family

Ra'ah. Ra'ah. Ra'ah.

Lo'laini's heart ached with every paper-thin bark of the lone baby seal crying into the empty ocean at La Jolla children's beach. She tugged on her grandmother's arm. "TuTu, is he okay?"

"Of course," Aninki smiled. "Mother seals nursing their young often plunge into the ocean to regulate their body temperature and to hunt. That little one just needs to be patient. Mom will arrive soon."

"I don't know," Aunt Emily whispered. "I've read that mother seals will sometimes abandon one of their twins when they don't have enough milk, or when the mother is disturbed or frightened, she may rush into the water and forget her young."

"We saw the mother and pup when we arrived this morning. She was nursing just one pup, and she did not look disturbed when she plunged into the water." Aninki smiled at Lo'laini.

Lo'laini and Aninki had arrived at La Jolla Shores at eight that morning to meet Lo'laini's aunts. They sat silently in a gazebo overlooking the children's pool at La Jolla shores, a beach famous for its blue-green waters and wildlife. Lo'laini leaned into the sea breeze. It cooled her neck and her arm, which was still in a cast from the car accident.

She searched the shore, expecting her father to walk across the beach and swoop her up, telling her his death was a terrible misunderstanding and that he had walked away from the accident. Instead, she saw nothing, but the sandy shores filled with gawking tourists taking pictures of seals.

She sat between her grandmother and estranged aunt. She had so many questions that the adults didn't want to answer. She still didn't understand why she couldn't go back to Hawaii to live with her grandmother, Tutu. She'd loved her aunts as a child, but she hadn't seen them in ten years. She didn't know why her dad had not wanted her to reunite with them.

The tourists cheered as a sleek brown seal pierced the waves near the cove and wobbled over the bumpy mounds of sand toward the crying pup, who quickly snuggled against his mother's body, looking for a place to nurse as the mother seal looked indifferently at the cheering crowd.

Lo'laini smiled and whispered to herself, "Everyone in that crowd was wishing for the same thing."

"Of course," Aunt Emily said. "Everyone hurts when a baby cries."

Emily was round and soft with strawberry-blonde hair that would not rest quietly in the confines of her hair band as rogue curls sprang out from the sides of her ponytail. Her bangs hung in unruly curls across her forehead. She wore a simple blue dress with a light gray rain jacket. Her tempera paint-stained hands betrayed her profession as a kindergarten teacher. Her soft nurturing voice exemplified her teaching skill. It soothed Lo'laini, although she didn't want to admit it at that moment.

The baby seal diverted her and her aunt from their stilted conversation. When Aunt Emily first recognized Lo'laini, she ran across the street and pulled her into a suffocating hug. Aninki had to explain to Emily that Lo'laini didn't like anyone to hug her. Emily apologized and told them her sister, Sandra, was looking for a parking place, which everyone agreed would take a while at that time of day.

Emily sat next to Lo'laini and pulled out her phone. She showed Lo'laini her baby pictures from sixteen years earlier, which embarrassed her. The baby seal crying broke through the tension.

Lo'laini took out her phone and typed, <*Where r u, girl, miss ya, miss ya so much*>

"Are you texting Karrie?" Aunt Emily asked.

Lo'laini quickly put down her phone. "Yeah, I'm sorry. I guess I should be talking to you."

"Not necessarily. You don't know me very well. Does this beach remind you of Hawaii?" Emily asked.

Lo'laini smiled. How did La Jolla Shores compare to Kahaluu Beach Park, where she grew up? La Jolla was pretty, but it was nothing like the beaches where Lo'laini swam with her father. Beneath La Jolla's blue-green waves were caves, rocks, sea grass, and brown and goldfish, but Kahaluu's waters brimmed with schools of multi-colored fish swimming between golden, pink, and purple reefs. *I guess all beaches are the same for Aunt Emily.*

"I don't know you well, Lo'laini," confessed Aunt Emily said. "But I wanted to know you. I... we ... I mean to say Sandra and I wanted to watch you grow up."

Lo'laini joined her aunt in gazing at the lacy patterns of white foam on the waves.

"We wanted to know you. We wanted to be a part of your life, Lo'laini." Emily put her hand on Lo'laini's back.

"I guess I knew what Dad said about you wasn't true."

Emily looked down at her hands. "What did he say about us?"

"Nothing. It doesn't matter." Lo'laini looked at her aunt's soft round face. Her face was sweet, and her green eyes were kind. She wasn't the same woman her dad described in his drunken rages or maybe she was. Lo'laini had no way of knowing. People often had two sides. Maybe her dad lied. Maybe Emily was lying. Maybe everyone lied.

"Is it foggy all the time in England?" Lo'laini asked.

"Not as much you Yanks say," Emily smiled, but Lo'laini didn't return it. Emily put an arm around her. Then she swiped her phone to show a freckled-faced school-aged boy with a plump red-haired toddler on his back.

"Here's a picture of your dad and me when we were younger. I loved him. He was my big brother, and I always wanted to be around him, even though he pushed me away. Who would want a ruddy tomboy baby sister tagging behind you when hanging out with your mates, eh?"

Emily giggled, "When I was little, he would carry me on his back and make horse noises. "We're going to conquer the world!" I would shout as I waved a cardboard sword over my head. "To the citadel! To the citadel!" he would shout as we ran through the kitchen and out the back door. I don't even think he knew what a citadel was. It must have been something he heard on the telly, but then things changed. He changed."

"When did he start drinking?" Lo'laini asked.

"Why talk about the past today?" Aninki asked with a worried look. "There's so much sadness. Let's talk about new beginnings."

"But I want to know, Tutu. All I've ever heard was my dad's side. Mom would never talk about it. I want to hear what someone else has to say about it. I want to know why Dad got drunk all the time."

Emily took a deep breath. "When he turned sixteen, he made some new friends, and everything changed. It hurt me because he became embarrassed of me in his teenage years, but I figured that was normal. When he started drinking, I knew that wasn't normal. Our dad drank a lot before he died, so I recognized the smell of alcohol on Dan's breath. One time, I came home and heard him yelling at our mum. I had never heard him raise his voice to her before. I guess she found his stash of booze under his bed. I came home and Mum had lined up his old wine bottles on the dining room table, and Dan was just standing there. "What about these, eh?" my mum shouted. "It killed your dad. You think it won't' kill you too? I saw what alcohol did to my dad and my husband. I don't want to lose my boy to this bleeding nonsense!" Daniel yelled back and said horrible things about her driving my dad away. I'd never heard him yell at anyone the way he yelled at her. I stepped in, thinking he'd stop for me, but then he stared angrily at me too."

"I remember him yelling at Tutu that way after my mom died," Lo'laini said.

"Tutu?" Emily asked.

"That's Polynesian for grandma." Lo'laini smiled at Emily. "Dad could get mean if he was cornered about his drinking. After he yelled at Tutu, he went after anyone who got between him and his drugs."

"You see," Emily said. "Not everything he said about his family was true. I loved him and tried to get him to stop. After a while, I had to accept that it wasn't that he didn't love me. It was that he loved the booze more. When someone got between him and his booze, it was always the same story," Lo'laini whispered to the ground. "He said people hated him because they were jealous that he had more fun, or they were frustrated with their lives, so they picked him apart. But no one had to pick his life apart. His life was falling apart because of the booze." She wiped away a tear.

"So, you don't believe everything he told you about us, eh?" Emily nudged Lo'laini with her elbow. "We're not as bad as he made us out to be."

"No. I knew it was booze talking when he said ugly things about his family. But he's not here to defend himself, so I don't think we should talk about it anymore." Lo'laini looked out at the beach again.

"He wasn't always like that, you know," Aunt Emily whispered as she wiped away a tear. "He was different growing up. He was smart, funny, and he had a lot of friends."

"He was like that before Mom died. He was wonderful to me sometimes, and I loved it when he made me laugh. The drugs made him stupid and scared, which is what getting stoned does, I guess." Lo'laini looked up.

The breathless figure of Aunt Sandra stood before her. "I had to park three blocks away. Maneuvering traffic in this crowd is an accomplishment indeed, not to mention that you lot drive on the wrong side of the road."

Lo'laini's two aunts were as different as anyone could imagine. Aunt Sandra was all pointy angles in her face and personality. She walked with the authority of a CEO. Her deep brown hair wove around a long-jeweled hairpin on the back of her head. She wore a tailored tweed suit that showed off her slender body. The light green silk blouse showed off her piercing blue eyes. Her makeup complimented her sculpted, angular face. Aunt Sandra had studied English literature in hopes of teaching, but her family needed a businessperson to take care of the family estate, so Sandra filled that role. She didn't look like someone you would want to challenge in the workplace.

Sandra surveyed Lo'laini's arm and neck cast and shook her head. "Did my idiot brother do that to you? I am so sorry,"

"Not so harsh, Sandra," Aunt Emily whispered. "Try to be a little more diplomatic."

"Diplomacy doesn't work, Emily. Not in this family. This rubbish has been going on for generations, and it's best to get it in the open. Especially now." Sandra reached for Aninki's hand. "I am so glad you were here to look after Lo'laini."

"She is my granddaughter. I could do nothing less," Aninki said.

Sandra lifted a paper cup to her lips. As she took a sip, she wrinkled her face. "Why can't the people in the States brew a simple cup of tea? Tea bags? Really? I've already accepted the fact that Western society has given up on the idea of loose tea brewed in a kettle, but I don't understand why someone would serve me lukewarm water in a flimsy cardboard cup when they have gallons of coffee pots brewing coffee. Why can't they set aside one kettle to brew a proper pot of tea?"

She tossed the cup in the trash with the authority of an executive rejecting an employee's substandard work. "I will have a proper cup of tea if I have to teach one of these so-called baristas how to prepare one."

Lo'laini had never known a woman who carried herself with the same authority as Aunt Sandra. When she'd walked across the boulevard, she'd stared at the oncoming car until it stopped.

Lo'laini loved her mother and her Tutu, but if one phrase described them, it would be 'gracious and hospitable,' and they tried to instill those qualities in her. She'd tried hard to have the same quiet, sweet spirits her mother and grandmother had, but it never came to her. But in Aunt Sandra, she saw something familiar, something that had already started to grow inside of her.

Aunt Sandra looked at everyone staring at her. "I'm sorry. It's ridiculous to get so angry at something so trivial. I guess it's Daniel's death and everything. All I'm asking for is a simple cup of brewed tea. It doesn't seem like it's too much to ask!"

"Come on, sis," Emily said. "We're in paradise. At the beach! Can't you just hang loose?"

"Emily, you know very well that I do not hang, and if I did, it would not be very loosely."

Sandra's confession brought an air of relief, and everyone laughed.

"There's a new coffee shop on Girard Avenue called Coffee, Tea, and Sweets. I think they have brewed tea," Lo'laini said.

Aunt Sandra smiled. "Shall we make the journey?"

Lo'laini jumped up beside Sandra and Emily, and Aninki followed. Suddenly, the day seemed lighter. Laughter and light conversation sprinkled their walk—until they reached the teashop. An extensive line trailed out the front door and down Girard Avenue. Sandra sighed when she saw the line.

"Sorry, Aunt Sandra," Lo'laini said. "These are the lines we have in La Jolla."

"Not much of a problem. Why don't your Aunt Emily and your grandmother Aninki find us a seat?" Sandra nodded her head at them. "We'll wait in line."

Aunt Sandra stood out from the crowd at the coffee shop. Her business attire contrasted with the tourists' t-shirts, shorts, and flip-flops or tennis shoes.

She unfastened the top two buttons on her teal silk blouse, which did little to help her to appear casual. "How long do you have to wear the casts?" Sandra asked as they took their place in line.

"The doctor said about five more weeks."

"I'm sorry for the way I talked about your father. I know you're still grieving him, as am I. I guess we all grieve differently."

Lo'laini nodded.

Sandra looked impatiently at the chattering tourists around her. "Sometimes I get angry at stupidity, especially when it's dressed up to look fashionable. The way I see it, my brother's lost his life in an addiction, which was wasteful and unnecessary," Sandra paused and bit her lip. "I hate ridiculous waste."

"I get angry sometimes, too, Aunt Sandra," Lo'laini whispered.

Sandra smiled. "Well then, let's get on with it. What would you and your grandmother like to drink this morning?"

"Hot chocolate for me and black coffee for Tutu."

"Right then."

Suddenly they were at the front of the line. Sandra faced a blonde surfer in his twenties. He wore swim shorts and a flowered t-shirt with flip-flops. He pushed back his stringy blonde hair, sniffed, and said, "Hey, babes. How can I do you?"

"Do me?" Sandra tried to ignore the faux pas of pushing back his hair while serving a customer. "You are not given permission to "do me" in any way, shape, or form, and please refrain from using any infantile terms when addressing me. I am a long way from wearing nappies and don't appreciate terms that may describe me as if I am still in one, but of course, you can take our orders."

"Uh, yeah. That's what I meant," he said.

"We will have two large coffees, one black and a hot chocolate." She leaned in and said, "I want you to listen carefully to me. I would also like a cup of brewed tea."

"Oh yeah," said the server. "We've got all kinds of tea."

"Please listen carefully. I do not wish for a soggy tea bag in lukewarm water brewed in a paper cup, mind you. I would like loosened tea brewed in boiling water. By boiling water, I mean water you have brought to a rolling boil in a teapot so it can brew tea and through a strainer into a proper cup."

"Uh... well... we don't have any teapots," he stammered.

"You don't have any teapots! You do realize the sign outside says Coffee, Tea, and Sweets. Don't you find it a tad incongruent to advertise tea and yet not possess a pot to brew the tea?"

"Yeah, well, I don't know what incongruent means."

"No doubt a tribute to the American school system," Aunt Sandra mumbled under her breath.

"Oh my gosh!" a teenage girl squealed from across the room. "Is that a British accent? That is *so* cute." She walked toward Aunt Sandra, but Sandra's cold stare made her retreat to her chair.

"Well, we got tea," said the server. "But it's in tea bags and in cups. Our water is pretty hot, so it won't be lukewarm or anything."

"Since I don't know the temperature of "pretty," I will trust that the water has been brought to a proper boil." Aunt Sandra rubbed her eyes. "What types of tea do you have?"

The young server's face brightened, and he began to recite a sales pitch that he had clearly memorized.

"We got this new stuff. People say they really like it. It's called Berry Delicious." He pulled out a transparent tea bag with dried blue and blackberries in it. "We heat fizzy mineral water with strawberries on the bottom, then add the tea bag."

Aunt Sandra examined the bag. "Excuse me if I am wrong, but I do not see any tea in there."

"No, like I said, it has berries."

"But I ordered tea, and what you have presented me is not tea." She leaned in and tapped her fingers on the counter. "Do you not see the dishonesty of calling this beverage tea? When you call something tea, one assumes the product contains *black tea*. Tepid fizzy water with berries is not what any reasonable person would expect when they order tea."

"Uh… well, we also have Lipton and Earl Grey if you want one of them."

"Since I have already had a disappointing encounter with Mr. Lipton, I shall commune with Lord Earl Grey this morning," Aunt Sandra said.

"What?"

"A cup of hot water with a bag of Earl Gray tea, please."

"Sure. What size? Venti, Grande, or petite?"

"Venti, Grande, or petite?" Aunt Sandra's rose in exasperation. "Do you realize the words you have used are not real words? They are not English, nor are they proper Italian, Spanish, and French words and by using them the way you have, you have, in effect, made yourself functionally illiterate in three languages!"

"Listen, lady," the man said roughly. "I only work here, and eleven dollars an hour is not worth this conversation."

Emily appeared and took her sister by the arm, turning her away from the server as she said, "Just a large cup of Earl Gray for my sister, please."

"Watch it. Mary Poppins's evil twin at table four," he said to one of the waiters.

Sandra turned around and lifted one eyebrow. "Apparently, English colonization did not have the desired effect of bringing civilization to this continent."

Emily blushed, "My sister, of course, is joking."

"Thank you, dear, for apologizing for the obvious."

Sandra asked a server where the facilities were. After a lengthy dialogue about the nonsensical custom of calling a room "bathroom" when it contains no bath on the premises, Sandra excused herself from the table.

The moment Sandra left, Lo'laini burst into laughter.

"It's not kind to laugh at someone else's idiosyncrasies," Tutu said.

"I'm not laughing at her. I'm laughing at the whole situation."

"I wouldn't blame you if you laughed at her," Aunt Emily said. "Sometimes it's hard for me to believe I'm related to her."

"Really? I can totally believe I'm related to her."

Aninki furrowed her brow. "Lo'laini, you would never speak to people in that disrespectful tone."

"But I want to. I want so badly," she laughed louder. "I'm sorry, but everything has been serious for so long. It feels good to laugh."

Emily smiled impishly. "I thought she would explode when the server brought out that bag of dried berries."

"I was sure the server was going to wet himself," Lo'laini said.

Emily looked up as the waitress arrived with their beverages. "I am sorry for my sister's behavior. She's had a rough time of it lately."

"Don't worry about it." She placed the drinks on the table. "Todd's a little too casual with the customers."

When she left the table, Lo'laini lifted her hot chocolate and said, "How good it feels to laugh today."

"It is the gift that God gives to help us get by." Aninki raised her coffee cup to touch Lo'laini's.

Aunt Sandra returned to the table and scooted into the booth. "I hope I am not the cause of this merriment."

"No," Aninki said. "Life is."

"And laughter helps us get through it." Emily lifted her coffee cup.

"Well, then. To get through it." Sandra joined the toast.

Lo'laini blew the whipped cream from the top of her hot chocolate and sipped. The warm liquid ran down her throat and warmed her stomach. She leaned over and rested her head on Aninki's shoulder, then reached across the table and took Aunt Sandra's hand. Aunt Sandra was startled, but then her face softened, and she squeezed Lo'laini's hand.

†

Chapter Three

Karrie's Hope: The Perfect Dress

"I guess there's no hiding it anymore." Isabella put her hands on her rounded belly as she surveyed herself in the breakroom's full-length mirror.

"So, stop trying," Alejandro said as he nuzzled up behind her, wrapping his arms around her and placing his hands over her belly. "*Mi bella esposa,*" he whispered in her ear.

"*Mi esposo halagador.*" Isabella giggled as she pushed Alejandro away.

"Oh... ah... excuse me," Karrie stammered as she opened the door. "I'm sorry."

"No need to be sorry." Isabella removed her badge and put on a cardigan. "It's your breakroom."

Alejandro looked at Isabella. "My wife was just going home to get some rest."

"Rest? How do you expect me to rest when you won't do what I ask?" Isabella picked up her purse. "I'll rest when I know you've read those Excel sheets I prepared for our taxes."

"Don't worry." Alejandro headed toward the door. "I'll get to it when I get to it."

"Don't worry. Don't worry. Until it's tax time, and you're throwing up your hands in confusion because you didn't keep track of our expenses and profits."

Alejandro shrugged. "Time to go back to work." He blew a kiss on Isabella.

"Karrie, can I give you a ride home?" Isabella asked as her husband went through the double doors onto the main floor.

"I guess," Karrie said while looking at her phone. "But I'm not going home. I'm going to Fashion Valley Mall to pick up my prom dress."

"Your young man finally asked you?" Isabella opened the door to the parking lot.

"Yeah," Karrie smiled and put away her phone.

"Was that a text from Lo'laini? What does she say?"

"Not much." Karrie closed her locker and picked up her purse. "I'm reading between the lines, but she doesn't seem to be doing well with her aunts."

"That's got to be rough." They walked through the alley to Isabella's Jeep.

"I don't know how I'd feel about leaving everything for a new country to live with people who had only known me when I was a little girl." Karrie climbed into the passenger seat.

"Especially after losing your father," Isabella sighed as she backed out and started toward the highway. "You know, that's what my mom did."

"Your mom? Did she lose her dad?"

"She lost everything. Her husband, her home, and her extended family. An army raided her village during the 1990 Guatemalan civil war, and she walked away with me on her back. She walked from Guatemala to the Mexican-Arizona border to ask for asylum in the United States."

"How old were you?"

"Just a month old."

"I thought you were Mexican."

"So did I until I was eighteen. Mom never talked about it. I knew we were immigrants because I was old enough to remember getting our citizenship. It was a big day. Me and my mom went down to the courthouse and took the vow, then had lunch at Denny's afterward."

"You didn't know you were Guatemalan? Didn't an official say anything about it?"

"I was little, and there were a lot of things I didn't understand about that day." Isabella shrugged. When I was in school, my mom spoke Spanish differently than some of my classmates' moms. It wasn't until I was sick my freshman year of college that I heard my mom tell a doctor we were Guatemalan." Isabella pulled into the Fashion Valley parking lot. She rubbed her stomach. "This little one is active today. He's a kicker."

"How does it feel?" Karrie looked at Isabella's belly.

"To be an immigrant?"

"To have life growing inside you."

"Ahhhh." Isabella smiled. "It feels good right now but a bit uncomfortable." Isabella pulled into a parking spot and turned off the car.

"You know, when I met Alejandro at Brown University and he told me he wanted to run a restaurant, I thought he was a dreamer. I wanted to get away from him."

Karrie laughed. "What happened? How did he change your mind?"

"He didn't change my mind. I changed it. He started showing up at church, and we had lunch after, first with some of our college friends but then alone. We had long talks and great walks after class. Romantic, silly stuff." Isabella rolled her eyes. "And then he made me kak'ik."

"Kak'ik?"

"It's Guatemalan turkey soup with roasted vegetables and lots of garlic in a sweet-sour sauce. When I tasted that soup— wow! I knew he wasn't a dreamer."

"Did you tingle? Sometimes when I'm with Tom, it feels as if my heart will burst out of my chest. I feel like I'm on fire when Tom and I are alone."

"Alejandro and I were a slow burn, which started from friendship." Isabella looked at Karrie. "Blazing fires are exciting to watch, but if you get too close to them, you get burned. You can't relax in their warmth. A smoldering fire will keep you warmer longer."

Karrie smiled as she opened the car door.

"Before you leave, I wanted to talk to you about something. You know Alejandro and I had a tiny house built so I could take care of my mother before she moved into assisted living."

"I saw it at the Christmas party last year."

"We'd like to make it available to you while you attend San Diego City College in the fall."

"That's nice, but I think my mom and I need to stick together right now. She needs my salary to help with rent and—"

"Karrie, I know you give half your salary to your mom for rent, but when school starts, you're going to need that money for other things. Besides, you should be able to buy nice things for yourself now and then."

Karrie's face flushed. "My mom made a lot of sacrifices for me when I went into foster care. She lost her house over that whole episode."

"She lost her house because she was defending your father, not because of you."

Karrie looked at the ground as she plucked at the door handle. "My mom needs me, Miss Isabella," Karrie whispered.

"I think your mom can take care of herself." Silence hung in the air as Karrie tapped on the door handle. "The house is available if you want it."

"Thanks." Karrie shut the door and ran toward Nordstrom's.

***

As Karrie entered Nordstrom's, perfumed air soothed her warm face. "Uptown Girl" played over the loudspeaker. Karrie's pace quickened to the beat as the stress of her workday melted away. She walked past perfumes and make-up counters, then brushed her fingers against the racks of pastel dresses glowing in yellows, pinks, and floral prints.

She passed through the clothes until she reached the back counter. Her eyes scanned the racks in the back by the dressing room while she waited to speak to a salesclerk.

"Can I help you?" asked an employee as she opened a new register.

"I'm looking for a dress that a salesclerk put away for me last month."

"Your name?"

"Karrie O'Leary."

The woman looked at a list on the counter. "A floor-length A-line/princess sleeveless satin gown. I'll be right back." She retreated into the dressing room and then came out with Karrie's dress wrapped in a garment bag. "Why don't you take a closer look at this dress before you pay for it." She passed the dress to Karrie and whispered, "Did you notice the stain on the back and a tear in one of the pleats?"

"Yes," Karrie said, taking the dress. "I also noticed it's eighty percent off."

"You might want to try it on anyway," she said in a motherly tone. "I'll stand behind the door if you need help zipping it up."

Karrie stepped into the dressing room and changed into her dress. It fell gracefully over her body. She waved her hand over the door to beckon the sales lady inside. Karrie's complexion glowed against the pink satin that gently cupped her top and descended into a beaded bodice that snuggly hugged her waistline. Pleats of pink satin cascaded to the floor.

Karrie didn't simply look beautiful in the dress. She was eloquent and womanly.

The salesclerk smiled. "Maybe a damp cloth with a little bit of detergent will get that stain out. And no one will notice a few stitches in a pleat."

Karrie swayed to one side. The skirt fanned out with a gentle swish against the floor.

"And the hair?" The salesperson twisted Karrie's reddish-blonde curls into a French twist. "You'll be the perfect princess. Cinderella would blush enviously in your presence."

"A perfect dress for a perfect night. That's all I want, just one perfect night."

✝

Chapter Four

Agostina's Journey: A Nursing Home

Claremont, 2019

"Mamá." Isabella touched her mother's knee. "Me conoces? No, me reconoces. Es Isabel. Tu pequeña."

Her mother stared blankly. Warm tears gathered in Isabella's eyes. She picked up her mother's heavy arm, opened her fist, and placed her hand on her bulging belly.

"Ver? Este es tu nieto," Isabella wept. "Your grandchild."

Agostina stared at the young woman in front of her. She didn't know her.

Her arm ached. When the young professional woman in from of her picked it up, it tingled with needles. Why was her arm so heavy?

Earlier that morning, a woman with a glowing face and sweet voice had roused Agostina from her comfortable covers and dressed her while singing "De Colores." The melody warmed her heart, but it also tortured her because the melody sparked a memory, a faint picture that she couldn't grasp.

"Your daughter is coming today." The woman smiled as she brushed Agostina's hair into a neat bun.

Agostina shook her head.

"Why do you say no when someone who loves you so much wants to see you?"

"No, no, no." Agostina pleaded with the nurse. She did not want to leave the security of her room. She did not want to dress and have people stare at her. She couldn't name the people, places, or things around her. She knew people expected something of her, but she didn't know what, so she nodded when people spoke to her, even when she didn't understand what they were saying.

She remembered a time when her hands were not so heavy, and she remembered falling in the garden, but she could not remember anything else—and she no longer wanted to try. Instead, she stared at the changing sunlight that spilled through the window shades into oblong shadows onto the carpet. It soothed her. She wanted to stay in her room and keep company with the shadows.

She resisted as the nurse helped her to the wheelchair. "Isabella, your daughter is waiting."

She remembered she had a baby named Isabella. She was such a good baby. Agostina had swaddled her in a tightly woven colored blanket. The blanket her mother had given her on her wedding day. Agostina used to strap Isabella to her back and take her into the sugarcane fields where she worked with her husband, Abisai. When she bent over to pick up sugar cane shoots that fell to the ground, her fellow workers told her that Isabella smiled at the sun.

"My little girl will be a great ray of sunlight to everyone she meets," Agostina would boast at the Sunday night meals she shared with their small Pentecostal church that met in a white and green house they had transformed into a chapel on the edge of town.

"God has anointed her smile." The other women would agree.

Life could be challenging in Kano. It took a sturdy back and quick arms to meet the quota expected from the workers, but Agostina had both, along with a beautiful baby and a husband who loved her. Kanois was her home. It was unthinkable to live in any other place.

Her mother used to say, "Kanois is the place for honey because it is surrounded by sugar cane," when she came in from the fields. Then she would scoop Agostina into her arms and say, "That's why the people here are so sweet."

The money wasn't much, but it was enough. The owner of the farm was stern, but Agostina and her husband had managed to stay on his good side by being the most productive workers in the field.

"A gift for you, beautiful!" Abisai tossed a small shrub to her in the middle of the workday. She caught it and pressed the peppermint leaf to her nose.

Abisai started bringing her bouquets of peppermint leaves when she was in Sunday school. Her family's house had been built by open sewage, and when Abisai learned the curly-haired girl in the back pew was getting sick because of the smell, he began leaving peppermint leaves on her seat and then on her family's front porch in the cool of the evening as he sat with her and watched the sun disappear. So, no one was surprised when Agostina wove them into her hair on her wedding day when she married the skinny kid who picked fresh peppermint every morning.

They set up home in a little pink adobe house that had been in Abisai's family for generations. He buffed the walls to a pearly yellow, and Agostina adorned them with brown and red glass mosaic tiles her grandfather had given her as a wedding gift. She sectioned off the kitchen from the bedroom with a colorful tapestry her mother and sisters had given her.

A jerk from her wheelchair brought Agostina back from the memory of Kanoto to the nursing home. The light pink and green lobby with pastel-colored floral sofas buzzed with the humming of a nearby television.

"My home was fresh with the smell of life, not medicine and lying flowers!" Agostina sneered as she hit a small table, knocking over a basket of plastic flowers.

"I'm sorry." Isabella pulled the wheelchair out of reach of the table.

"Mama, what are lying flowers?"

"Plastic flowers." Agostina looked at the table. "Plastic flowers for this plastic life I now live." She looked in desperation at Isabella. "My life wasn't always plastic."

Isabella smoothed her mother's hair, and Agostina closed her eyes. Her mind drifted back to the Easter morning she had last felt at home—that horrible morning when she left Kano.

Easter morning worship had beckoned her out of bed before the sun came up. She cut fresh fruit for breakfast and was making flatbread while laughter floated from the bedroom as Abisai lifted Isabella over his head and shouted, "The magical flying baby, such strength! Such might!"

Agostina's heart warmed as she flattened the tiny balls of white dough and pressed them onto the open fire stove in the middle of the kitchen. Heat puffed the dough, creating brown and black dots. Once they were ready, she wrapped the flatbread in a warm cloth. She glanced at Isabella and Abisai. Nothing could trouble her peppermint paradise.

Civil war had raged in Guatemala for thirty years, and young men often disappeared in the night. The army forced them to give their lives for a cause they neither believed in nor understood. For several months, she'd heard rumors of people leaving all they possessed to travel north, but that was unthinkable to Agostina.

Agostina thought Abisai was safe. He was a skinny farm worker who wrote poetry and sang ballads. No army would want him. She would not lose him to them.

Agostina opened her arms to Isabella as Abisai bounced her on the bed. "Church in two hours."

"What is this?" She picked up some documents. "Important papers on the floor?"

"Visas, passports, and train tickets my brother mailed me." Abasi laughed as he poked and tickled Isabella. He stood up while holding Isabella upside down; her arms fell over her head as she squealed in laughter. "I was looking at them when this child attacked me."

"I better keep these with me, or they will soon be lost." Agostina placed the papers in a cloth bag.

"I would feel better about visiting my brother if you were coming with us." He gently rubbed Agostina's back and whispered in her ear, "I would feel so much better with my family near me."

Agostina shrugged Abasi's hands off her shoulders. "I do not know that place, and when people go to the States, they never come back. I don't want to leave my home."

"My heart is hanging in your hands." Abasi wrapped his arms around her.

"Your heart is in God's hands." Agostina gently kissed him. "Do you remember where I am going this morning?"

"Yes," he laughed, breaking away to grab a piece of fruit from the table. "You're going to meet the other women in a small cave you found in the canyon."

"It will be beautiful." She swaddled Isabella in the blue, yellow, and red zigzag cloth.

"I will see you in two hours." Abisai gently kissed her cheek.

The women of the church met to pray before the service. One of them had discovered a small cave behind the sugar cane field, which gave them the idea to have an Easter pageant. After the minister's message, one of the women would run in and say, "The tomb is empty! Jesus has risen!" The congregation members would follow her to the cave, where they would find a grave cloth on a flat stone bed. The women would lead the congregation in songs before gathering back at the church for a small meal.

An air of excitement filled the cave as the women swept out the cobwebs, dusted the floor, and adorned it with flowers and chairs. Agostina laid a cloth on the floor and set Isabella on her tummy. Agostina called the woman to sit next to her as she tore off tortillas and dipped them in a plate of beans Bibiana, the pastor's wife, had brought for breakfast. They laughed with excitement as they anticipated their pageant.

A loud bang interrupted their laughter. Agostina scooped up Isabella as she let out a cry. The women's quieted and then agreed it was nothing more than a backfiring car. Isabella calmed down as her mother gently bounced her. Nervous laughter broke their silence, and they began their meal again.

A thunderous bang shook the walls. Suddenly the women became aware of the smell of smoke and the cries of women and children from the town. The women stared at each other, consumed by a realization. It had happened to other villages before. Armies raided and leveled their towns to dust while accusing the villages of conspiring with one side or another in the endless civil war.

Azule, the youngest of them, stood and ran toward the opening of the cave. Bibiana pulled her down.

"My children—" she gasped.

"Are no more," Bibiana said, rocking the woman in her arms.

Isabella began to whimper. Agostina lifted her blouse so she could nurse. All the women huddled on the floor of the cave throughout the day into night, praying in muffled cries.

When the sun rose the next day, the roar of jeeps rolled by. They waited another day before they left the safety of the cave.

Gunpowder and fire had blackened their pink, green, blue, and white adobe houses and turned them into shells. They wandered among the ruins, looking for lost loved ones.

"They must have buried the bodies to cover their crime," Bibiana whispered. "There should be more bodies than this."

Agostina ran toward the end of town, her eyes resting on the charred shell of her peppermint house. She ran inside. Maybe they had not taken him. Maybe he had hidden.

The glass and clay tiles and her family's tapestry lay in a heap on the floor. She picked up the charred cloth and folded it. A shot of hope sprang through her body when she saw the familiar legs and torso sticking out from beneath their bed.

She fell to her knees and shook his body. There were no visible wounds on his back or legs. She frantically pulled on his legs, dragging his body from beneath the bed. She could see blood clots on the top of his neck. With one great heave, she dragged him further out and, in horror, realized that his neck had no head.

"Abisai!" Agostina tried to scream but felt a hand cover her mouth and pull her back. She could hear Isabella crying in the distance. Then she heard Bibiana whisper, "Quiet. The trees have ears."

Agostina woke up in the cave; the women were talking in quiet whispers. The army would be back. They had to leave. One of the women had a cousin who worked on another plantation one hundred miles north. It was far, but they could make it. The village was small enough that the army could not bother it.

"Will you come, Agostina?"

"No," Agostina said, reaching down into her purse, fingering the visas and passports. "I have another option."

Isabella started whimpering.

Agostina picked her up and rocked her. "Don't cry my little one. Don't cry, Isabella."

"Mama, you know me!" The adult women's voice brought her back to the present. Isabella's face brightened when Agostina said her name. Agostina looked blankly at the professional-looking woman who had been crying and holding her hand.

"No, not you. My daughter. My baby." Agostina looked at the nurse. "Could you please take me back to my room?"

✝

Chapter Five

Sandra's Torture: Ungraspable Faith

"This is my church," Lo'laini proudly said as she opened the glass doors to let her aunts and Tutu inside.

"Lo'laini!" Deanna squealed from behind the reception desk as she ran around and hugged Lo'laini. "I'm sorry. I keep forgetting you don't like hugs."

"Mrs. Wright." Lo'laini freed herself and pointed toward her aunts and grandmother. "This is Aunt Sandra, Aunt Emily, and my grandmother, whom I call Tutu, but you can call her Aninki."

Tutu extended a hand to Mrs. Wright. "Thank you so much for letting Lo'laini swim in your pool. She has told me many times that you had her over for lunch after church."

"It was no trouble." Deanna shook Aninki's hand and then Lo'laini's aunt's hands and was slightly startled at Sandra's firm handshake. "Lo'laini and Karrie are such well-mannered girls, and we love having them in our home. I am so sorry for your loss."

"He's in a better place," Emily said.

"A place where he can't do any more harm," Sandra said.

"I know you're here to see Pastor Mike." Deanna returned to the reception desk. "He's finishing a meeting with the senior pastor. He asked if you could wait for him in the sanctuary." She pushed a button that allowed them to enter the office area, then led them down a hall to the main sanctuary.

They entered a white brick rectangular room bathed in purple light that poured through twelve blue-and-red checkered stained-glass windows. Twenty-four wooden pews faced a platform with several oversized chairs behind a podium. A cross in a yellow frame hung above the platform. To the side of the cross were four sets of copper organ pipes that descended from greatest to smallest as they stretched toward the ceiling. Beneath the cross, five rows of blue chairs in a half circle faced the pews.

Aninki and Emily sat in the back pews while Sandra stood at the back of the room.

Lo'laini pointed at the platform. "That's where our preacher preaches and those chairs in the back? That's where our choir sings."

"It must be a large choir," Emily said. "Are they any good?"

"I don't know." Lo'laini sat next to her grandmother. "I usually go to the gym for the contemporary service. We have a band that plays for our worship service. Dad went to the service in the sanctuary."

"How long did he go to church?" Sandra asked, looking down at her fingernails.

"About a year after, he sobered up. He was going to an Alcoholics Anonymous group, which also meets here."

"This room is pretty, but it seems rather stark to me," Emily sighed. "I can't wait for you to see the churches in England. There are such beautiful cathedrals there." She got up and squeezed herself between Lo'laini and Aninki, then pulled out her phone and swiped through pictures. "Here is Saint Paul's Cathedral in London." She swiped to a domed white building with a golden cross that crowned the cathedral. It looked more like a government building than a church. "And here is Westminster Abbey." She swiped again to an ivory building with two towers that stretched toward heaven.

"It looks like a castle," Lo'laini said.

"A little." Emily nudges Lo'laini with her elbow. "But the queen doesn't live there." She swiped again. "My favorite is All Saints Church in Sheepy Magna in Leicestershire."

The church contained a row of stained-glass windows that portrayed biblical characters framed by pomegranates, flowers, and leaves.

The windows with one-dimensional depictions of Jesus and his disciples mesmerized Lo'laini. "Wow, they're beautiful."

Her aunt handed her the phone so she could take a closer look. Jesus posed with his hands outstretched as if beckoning the viewer to climb into the window and stand with him. Two disciples stood next to Jesus, looking back at him in bewilderment. Behind Jesus, an emerald tree bloomed against a piercing blue sky. What entranced Lo'laini the most were the multicolored haloes surrounding each face.

"Those are William Morris-stained glass windows. People say the colors are so beautiful they are almost musical."

"Why did he make their halos different colors?" Lo'laini asked, enthralled by the picture.

"I don't know." Emily wrinkled her nose. "Probably symbolic. Jesus's halo is red for his blood, probably, and Peter's halo is purple for... I don't know. Maybe royalty... I can't figure out the reason for the gold one, but aren't the colors pretty?" Emily took back her phone and swiped to more pictures.

"Did my dad go to any of these churches?"

"No, dear," Sandra said from the back of the room. "We went to a small country church near our home where we grew up, and later, when he had a type of conversion, he attended a church that looked much like this one."

Lo'laini smiled.

Sandra sighed, digging her heel into the plush carpet. "Another lost cause."

"There is so much I want to show you in the UK," Emily said. "It's your heritage, you know. Here's the London Bridge, the Tower of London, and the Palace of Westminster."

"Is that where the queen lives?" Lo'laini asked.

Emily giggled, "Oh, no. That's where governmental heads meet, like your Congress." She ran her finger affectionately down Lo'laini's face. "Oh, little one, I must teach you about your own history."

Sandra noticed Aninki's face harden with Emily's last remark. She tried to catch her sister's eye to silence her, yet Emily continued.

"These are Buckingham Palace and Windsor Castle."

"The royal family owns them, and sometimes they live there, but the queen inherited other castles from her family, such as," Emily said as she swiped her phone again. "The Balmoral Castle and the Sandringham House."

Emily looked at Lo'laini's puzzled face. "The idea of the monarchy must seem foreign to you."

"A monarchy is not foreign to Lo'laini," Aninki said. "I told you when you came to my house that her grandfather taught her about the Hawaiian monarchy. She knows about Queen Lydia Kamakaeha Liliuokalani, who worked hard for our country. She organized schools and advocated education for the children of Hawaii while serving as a diplomat to President Cleveland and Queen Victoria before foreigners disposed of her in 1893."

"By the missionary party led by Sanford Dole?" Sandra stepped closer to them.

"Yes!" Aninki turned around to face Sandra. "I see you've done some research since we last talked."

"A little. The picture your husband painted was stunning."

"She was a stunning woman," replied Aninki.

"Doesn't it bother you, as a person of faith, that it was the missionary party that disposed your queen and helped the United States annex Hawaii? The same people who brought you Jesus exploited your country. I made a horrible joke about colonization at the coffee shop, and I'm sorry. I was wrong, but when I read about how your country was annexed, it angered me. I don't see how it couldn't bother you. They brought you a white man's religion and took away your self-rule."

"Wait a minute. You visited my grandma's house and talked? What about?" Lo'laini looked at Aninki. "I wish someone would have told me."

"It was a boring grown-up talk, nothing you need to worry about." Emily smiled at Lo'laini.

"You must learn more Hawaiian history before you lecture someone who has lived it." Aninki's eyes grew hard. "The missionary party primarily included businessmen and descendants of the missionaries. If you think I am unaware of my country's exploitations and struggles with Anglo-American commerce, you are sorely mistaken. It is a complicated history. No internet search can tell you the whole story."

"Let me make this clear to you, Sandra. No missionary gave me Jesus. God gave me Jesus. He used imperfect instruments, and I have reflected on that history all my life. I do not lay the short-sighted human mistakes at Jesus's feet."

"Christianity isn't white man's religion, Aunt Sandra. It was born in Palestine, so you could say it was started by brown people."

"It was started by God." Aninki smiled at Lo'laini.

"Why didn't you tell me you guys met?" Lo'laini started to cry. "Did you meet because you were sure Dad would fail?"

"You already had too much on your plate," Aninki said. "It was a conversation I needed to have with your aunts alone."

"I'm sorry. I shouldn't have brought it up." Sandra turned toward Lo'laini. "I learned your grandfather was an accomplished man, and your grandmother loves her family very much."

"We are here to remember Daniel," Emily said. "Let's not forget that."

"This was his church." Lo'laini walked over and hugged her grandmother.

"Yes." Sandra closed her eyes and took a deep breath. "His church. His conversion." She walked to the wall and leaned her head against it. "I don't like being in churches."

"That's quite obvious." Aninki look compassionately looked at Sandra. "Do you need to take a walk? We can plan the service if you need to take some time."

Sandra's eyes filled with tears, and she clenched her teeth. "I don't need a walk. I need to understand. I grew up in the church, and I'm certain my father believed, but the booze got him too. Then Daniel had this conversion, and everyone was so happy, but…" Sandra clenched her teeth and started to sob. "It didn't work, did it? It didn't bleeding work!"

"I think it worked," Lo'laini whispered.

"Sandra, we're in church," Emily said, trying to calm her sister.

"No!" Sandra stepped away from Emily. "Aninki is in church, and Lo'laini—bless her heart—is in church, and you, dear sister, are at least aesthetically in church—"

"I think it goes deeper than that," Emily said, sitting down again.

"I'm in a torture chamber! I am viewing a faith I cannot grasp. It keeps knocking at my door while I keep losing the ones I love. It's like water that slips through my fingers."

"I'm sorry to intrude." Pastor Mike stepped into the room. "If you'd like more time to talk, I can come back."

"No..." Sandra wiped her eyes. "There's nothing to talk about."

"Sandra," Aninki whispered. "I am sorry we were sharp with each other."

She waved her hand, pushing Aninki's words away. "You were correct. I shouldn't have used your history to express my anger. Of course, I am wrong. Especially as it isn't my history."

"Sandra, if you would allow me, I'd like to tell you about Daniel's faith." Pastor Mike sat on the back pew near Sandra.

"No, necessary. I am wrong, of course." Sandra walked toward the door. "I think Aninki was right. I need a walk. Of course, we'll pay for everything."

"I can help pay for my son-in-law's funeral," Aninki said.

"Yes, yes, of course. I was wrong, didn't mean to offensive." Sandra forced a smile. "I think I saw an ice cream shop around the corner. I rather fancy a cup of sherbet right now."

As Sandra left, she called over her shoulder, "You make plans, and we'll meet at the ice cream shop later."

Chapter Six

Aninki's Loss

And her Epiphany

Pastor Mike asked Lo'laini to share about her father's conversion and struggle with addiction. Exhausted by the previous argument, Aninki listened to her granddaughter's testimony about her father.

Aninki's mind wandered back to the day she had met with Sandra and Emily to talk about Lo'laini's custody arrangements. Sandra had sent her an email saying that she wanted to talk about the situation with Lo'laini and her father.

She was still mourning her daughter's death, and the idea of Lo'laini being in foster care unsettled her. Initially, she had applied to social services so Lo'laini could live with her. When she discovered Daniel was working to reconcile with Lo'laini, she pulled back based on the social worker's advice. The social worker thought the case with Daniel was promising and asked Aninki not to interfere by applying for custody.

"Taking Lo'laini back to Hawaii might interfere with the reconciliation process," the worker said over the phone Aninki wanted to make a case for her taking custody of Lo'laini, but the social worker made sense.

"We have to give these two a chance to bond again. Taking Lo'laini to Hawaii would make visitations impossible for her father. He wants to be in his daughter's life again, and you must know that Lo'laini wants to be with her father."

Yes, the social worker had been correct on that account. Almost from birth, Lo'laini gravitated toward her father. To everyone's surprise, Lo'laini picked up her father's British accent and carried herself with his authority and confidence. Naturally athletic, she and her father had so much in common. She took to water sports easily, and every Saturday, she and her father spent the day scuba diving and snorkeling at the local beaches.

For a moment, Aninki thought she could move to California to take custody of Lo'laini while her father cleaned himself up, but she couldn't afford to leave her business. It seemed the best decision was to allow Lo'laini to stay in foster care, but after Sandra's call, Aninki began to doubt her decision.

Aninki took a week off work to prepare for the aunts' arrival. She bought English breakfast tea and made coconut shortbread cookies. She had her cottage in Kaneohe, Hawaii, professionally cleaned. It wasn't grand, but it was situated between her church and her shop—for business she had inherited from her parents and built u twenty years before her husband passed away.

She painted her cottage walls light pink. Blue light reflected from the sea glass mobiles hanging in her windows. A blue-and-yellow Hawaiian tapestry hung above a white leather sofa. The women of her church had given her the tapestry when Mai was born.

Pictures of her young child surrounded the tapestry—images taken before cancer had betrayed Mai's body, eating away her hope and optimism. Pictures of Aninki's strapping young husband also hung there, and, of course, photos of herself when she was slender and willowy.

Aninki's home had always been a refuge for her. In the hungry years when her husband first taught at the university, Aninki's home was comfortable and clean. In more prosperous times, laughter and jokes filled it. But in the past few years of grief and loss, it had become a restful place. She wanted it to be a fortress against her granddaughter's aunts' intrusion. She didn't like feeling resentful. It seemed ugly and against her personality. She did her best to create an atmosphere of serenity to guard against the chaos she felt looming on the horizon. She opened the sliding glass doors to let the sea breeze carrying the smell of gardenias and plumeria from her terrace garden into the living room.

When Emily and Sandra entered her house, they brought their own tense atmosphere, which settled over Aninki's home.

Aninki welcomed them and tried to direct them to her sofa. Both sisters seemed uneasy in Ainki's home, but Emily was better at disguising it. Sandra moved toward the window.

"How lovely! How quaint!" Emily examined the window dressing and the chimes. Then, moving toward the sofa, she smiled and said, "These must be pictures of Lo'laini's mother."

"Yes." Aninki smiled. "That's my little girl, and holding her was my life's companion, Aheahe, Lo'laini's grandfather. He was a history professor at the University of Hawaii. He passed away ten years ago."

"I am sorry," Emily whispered.

"You have lost two relatives in the past decade?" Sandra's face softened.

"Three," Aninki said. "First my husband to heart disease, then my daughter to cancer, and then my granddaughter when her father moved her to California."

There was an awkward moment of silence.

"Lo'laini is the topic of our meeting today," she said. "So, let's move into the kitchen where we can have a cup of tea and take the edge off a very painful subject."

Both aunts obeyed as if they were two schoolgirls.

Aninki's living room opened to a spacious yellow kitchen. It had a bamboo table with a glass top in the middle. Aninki had already set out a porcelain teapot with mugs and saucers. The fragrance of hot tea and shortbread filled the room. Sandra and Emily sat at the table.

Once again, the pictures on the wall drew Emily's eyes away from the business at the table and into Aninki's pictorial family timeline that she had displayed on her light peach and yellow-tinted walls. Photographs of Mai and Lo'laini flowed gracefully from Lo'laini's birth to her high school years. A plump baby girl grew into a strong and athletic woman. The line of pictures showed Mai growing paler and frailer with time. Daniel appeared in only a few pictures, but he seemed to be a secondary figure. It was hard to tell whether that was the decision of the photographer or Daniel, but he seemed to be standing always on the side or in rear of each photograph. With each picture he stood further away from his wife and daughter, becoming more detached within each picture.

Aninki poured tea as Sandra pulled a large pile of papers from her briefcase.

"Tea first," Aninki said in a soft voice.

Sandra set down the papers and took a sip of tea. Her eyebrows raised as her shoulders relaxed. She took a second sip of warm tea. Well-brewed tea reminded Sandra of home and lazy Saturday mornings. She rested the mug against her jaw. As she relaxed, she looked over Aninki's shoulder at a portrait of a dignified Hawaiian woman dressed in a white Victorian gown with feathers lining her collar and a cream sash across her shoulder and waist. "Who is the majestic woman in that portrait, Aninki?"

"That is Queen Lydia Kamakaeha Liliuokalani. She was the last sovereign of Hawaii. My husband painted it when our daughter was born."

"She seems to be a formidable woman," Sandra said, taking another sip of tea.

"She was," replied Aninki. "I wish more people knew about her. She was a powerful woman who governed well and adapted to impossible situations to keep her government. As I told you, my husband was a historian. The queen was the subject of his doctoral thesis. I think he painted her as a role model for our young daughter."

"Did it encourage her?" Emily asked.

"I think it intimated her," Aninki said, offering the two sisters some cookies. "We don't get to create our children. They come with their own personalities." Aninki put down the cookie dish and gazed up at the painting. "My daughter was gracious, loving, and, in her own way, strong. But as far as historical figures go, I think Lo'laini matches the strength and Power of Queen Lydia Kamakaeha Liliuokalani and that there was more of Kaiulani in my daughter Mai than Liliuokalani."

"Who was Kaiulani?" Sandra asked.

"She was Liliuokalani's niece and heir. She was a gentle creature who stood up for her country but died too young," Aninki sighed. "No, if the spirit of Queen Liliuokalani lives in anyone in our family, it is Lo'laini."

"We don't wish to take Lo'laini from you, but I think we can offer her a better future," Sandra said. "I know you have done well, but we can give Lo'laini much more. Our family has a corporation set up from an ancestor's estate. It is Lo'laini's heritage, and we would like her to become a part of it. It'll just be a few years, then Lo'laini will be of age and can decide for herself where she will live, but for her formal education, we can take care of that."

The rest of Sandra's words tapered off in Aninki's ears, blurring into a melting, water-colored painting of nonsensical syllables. She wasn't prepared to take care of Lo'laini. Because of her husband's relationship with the college, Aninki could help Lo'laini through college, but she couldn't afford to do much more. She feared Lo'laini would lose her culture to these two English women.

Lo'laini already had a heritage—a Hawaiian heritage. Aninki had something inside of her to pass on to her granddaughter that the English women did not possess. The aunts clearly had histories that had set their teeth on edge, and Lo'laini already had been through enough with her father. She knew Lo'laini would be better off living with her in Hawaii, not with Daniel's sisters, but Aninki couldn't find the voice to contradict Sandra.

"Daniel may sober up, then Lo'laini could be reunited," Aninki said, but the cynical look on Sandra's face stopped her words.

Emily shook her head. "We appreciate your kind opinions about our brother, but we know him better." She took Aninki's hand, but Aninki withdrew and offered both sisters the cookies.

Maybe they were wrong about Daniel, but if they weren't, they could offer Lo'laini more security than she could. There had been too much insecurity in Lo'laini's life.

Sandra placed legal papers in front of Aninki. She stared blankly at them. Her hand trembled while she picked up the pen to sign them.

✝

Chapter Seven

Karrie's Dilemma

The Best and Worst Night

Ripple. Slash. Slush. The gentle current rocked the party boat on San Diego Bay. Karrie gazed at the dark sky sprinkled with stars like crystal jewels resting on dark velvet.

"Not a cloud in the sky," she whispered in Tom's ear as she rested her head, heavy with the fatigue of adolescent infatuation, on his shoulder. "This is a perfect night."

Both of their legs dangled off the side of the boat, occasionally touching the rock of the boat.

"Great idea, Mr. D," Tom shouted over his shoulder. "An after-prom cruise around San Diego Bay."

"No problem," Mr. Dalman said, pulling his wife closer to him. "It's a great date for us old people too."

"Karrie, I wish you would change into the shorts I brought," Mrs. Dalman said. "I hate to see your lovely dress ruined."

Karrie had gathered her wide satin skirt into a knot above her knees so her legs could sway to the rhythm of the boat.

"No way," Karrie said. "I paid two weeks' wages for this dress, and I know I'm not going to wear it again. I'm getting my full use out of it."

She pulled the pins out of her hair, and the sea wind brushed her hair back. "Thanks for the ride, Mr. and Mrs. D." Karrie threw her head back to smile at Josh's parents.

"Hey." Josh pulled in the sail to catch the night breeze. "It was my idea. I think I deserve some credit for this."

"Forgive us, your majesty." His dad bowed. "Let's all take a moment to recognize the genius of Josh Dalman."

Light laughter rippled through the group of friends.

"Perfect night," Karrie whispered again.

It hadn't begun as a perfect night. In fact, the beginning had been more like a nightmare. How could an evening that began so horribly end up so beautifully?

That morning, everyone at Karrie's work was excited about her prom date. Isabella scheduled Karrie for four hours, and she blocked out thirty minutes for the servers to help Karrie get ready.

After Karrie clocked out, she squealed in delight when she walked into the break room. Her co-workers had created a makeshift beauty salon to help her.

Margaret, the afternoon hostess, sat Karrie down and twisted her hair into a French twist, weaving together her sun kissed brown hair with some golden hair strands with her copper red ones. Next, Angelica and Anita laid out a kaleidoscope of foundations and eye makeup.

"Just a little," Karrie said. "I'm not used to a lot of makeup."

"It won't look like a lot the way we apply it." Angelical wiped a warm cloth over Karrie's face.

Anita tilted Karrie's chin up as she carefully examined her face. "First toner, then moisturizer, and a light foundation. To emphasize your cheekbones, a brownish pink blush, then…" She pulled out several makeup brushes. "We'll be ready for eyes."

Karrie couldn't believe her image in the mirror when they finished. She looked like one of those girls in her social media feed who advertised makeup and skin creams.

"Now for the crowning effect." Anita tilted Karrie's face down. "The eyelashes." She used tweezers to gently place a fine pair of eyelashes over Karrie's. Then she brushed mascara lightly over Karrie's eyelashes. "Now take a look, girl."

Karrie teared up.

"No tears." Angelica dabbed Karrie's face. "No makeup is ever really waterproof, you know."

Karrie hugged her workmates. "You guys are the best. "

Isabella called an Uber, so Karrie wouldn't have to take the bus home. When she opened the living room door, she found her mother asleep on the sofa. She had been sleeping more lately.

Karrie walked carefully around her mom and into her bedroom. She ran to the closet and pulled out her dress. Her hands trembled as she slipped out of her work uniform and into her prom gown. Her complexion glowed in pink silk. Her makeup and hair were perfect. She swayed to make her skirt fan out around her.

A loud bang startled Karrie.

"Open up! This is the police!"

Karrie stepped into the living room as her mother sat up, bewildered.

"Open up!"

Her mom stumbled to the door and opened it wide enough to see who was there. "What is it?"

"Are you Moriah O'Leary?"

"Yes."

"We have a report of drug sales from this residence." The police officer leaned into her mother's face.

Her mother stepped backward.

"Are you working tonight?" The younger officer leered at Karrie.

"You watch your mouth. That's my daughter, and she's going to the prom tonight."

"Listen, lady. We don't want to bug you or ruin anyone's evening. Let us search your place, and we'll be on our way."

"No! There are no drugs here. Who made the complaint? My ex got out of prison early. I bet it was him who called."

The police didn't answer.

"Besides, you need a warrant. I know my rights." Karrie's mother stood directly in front of the police.

"Not if we have probable cause, and with your record, we have probable cause."

Karrie felt a sting of betrayal. Her mother glanced at her, but Karrie went back into her room. She picked up the worn teddy bear the social worker had given her five years before. She gritted her teeth, holding back the tears as she remembered Anita's warning: nothing is waterproof.

"I can't let anyone leave this residence until we search it, so it will be easier on everyone if you let us do our jobs."

Karrie's mother nodded and defeatedly sat down on the couch. "I'll call in for a female assist." said the younger officer, pulling out his cell phone.

"What do you need a female assist for?" Karrie's mom stood up again.

"Everyone is going to have to search before they leave this apartment."

Karrie looked at her phone. *4:45.* The guys would arrive at 5 p.m. "Please, God, let Josh and Tom be late. Please let them put the wrong address into their GPS."

Ten minutes later, Karrie's mother called her into the living room. A Filipino policewoman with motherly eyes approached her. The woman's stature, voice, and mannerisms reminded Karrie of Lo'laini's grandmother, Aninki.

"I am sorry, Karrie," she said as she patted down Karrie's side and then her back. "I'm going to use the back of my hand to pat down your front, okay?"

Tears gathered in the corners of Karrie's eyes. She forced a smile and nodded.

"I hope things go better for you the rest of this evening."

The woman patted down Karrie's front. Karrie's eyes began to cloud. Something brown was blocking her vision. Oh, no! Her false eyelashes were falling off.

She turned to wipe her face and saw the open front door. Tom and Josh stood there with horrified faces. Tears fell uncontrollably down her face.

"We can fix this." The police officer turned Karrie's face toward hers. "My sister is in pageants all the time. I can make you better than before. Why don't you guys wait outside?" she said over her shoulder.

"You don't have to do this," the younger officer said.

She pointed a finger at his face. "Don't tell me what I have to do! This could have been managed better, and it's not the first time you and your partner have bullied women."

"We're not bullying anyone," the older officer said. "We had a report and probable—"

"Cause? Yeah, maybe I have probable cause to report this to the Community Review Board of Police Practices. Now let me make this right with this little girl while you go outside and talk to those scared kids or I'm going to make a storm that will follow you for the rest of your professional lives."

Karrie went to her room, where the police officer brushed her face with a cool washcloth. She reapplied her foundation. "Your mom's not you, little girl. Not everyone lives like this. Most people don't live from crisis to crisis."

"It's not my mom's fault."

"Maybe so, maybe not. Maybe you know something, and maybe you don't. Now close your eyes." The officer pressed the false eyelashes back into place. "Someone once told me that pain in life is inevitable, but living constantly in crisis is optional. There are better ways to live." She turned Karrie back toward the mirror. Her face shone bright pink, her makeup once again highlighted her Karrie flushed features. "Look at the girl in the mirror. That girl is going to find a better way to live."

Karrie left the apartment and walked to the complex's courtyard, where she saw Tom and Josh standing by their silver Mazda. Tom's face brightened when he saw her.

"We're riding in style," he said. "We're getting a police escort to the Spaghetti Factory."

"The Spaghetti Factory is my favorite restaurant!"

"That's not all." Josh pointed to the car. "We have a surprise for you inside."

The police officers opened the door, and Karrie got into the back seat. Tom slid in next to her and put his arm around her. Josh slid into the driver's seat and handed two large Orange Julius drinks to Karrie and Tom. She squealed in delight.

Josh pulled away from the curb. "We got to stop by my cousin's house first."

"Your cousin? Dude, you are taking your cousin to prom?" Tom laughed.

"What was I going to do? Lo'laini can't come, so I had to find someone."

"I guess that's true," said Karrie taking a big sip from her drink.

Josh looked in the rearview mirror at Karrie. "How is Lo'laini?"

"It's hard to say. She's been texting me, but I have to read between the lines with her. I think there's some conflict with her aunts." Karrie sighed. "I guess it's not weird to take your cousin if you're thinking about Lo'laini."

"Nope," Tom laughed. "Going to the prom with your cousin is definitely weird, no matter the circumstances. What a stereotype, taking your cousin because you can't get a date. Dude, are you sure you're not a hillbilly?"

"You'll like my cousin. Her name is Michelle, and she's smart and funny."

Karrie found out that Michelle was both of these things. While they were picking up Michelle, Josh told his uncle about the police officer's behavior. He suspiciously looked at Karrie and then he asked for details and walked out to talk to the officers.

Michelle put her arm around Karrie. "It's okay. We're going to have fun this evening."

Michelle was, in fact, smart and funny. She imitated movie stars on their prom dates, making each of them appear more awkward and nerdy.

"I'm going to choose the word for the day," she said as they walked toward the restaurant. Josh opened it for her. "It's incongruent."

From that moment, everyone tried to use the word in every sentence. Michelle pointed out that the streetcar in the middle of the restaurant was incongruent. Karrie said it was incongruent that the restaurant's carpet didn't match the walls.

When Tom said that the number of people around each table was incongruent, they booed him and said he didn't understand the game. When Josh said being at the prom without Lo'laini was incongruent, they joined in a sympathetic *aww* and put their arms around him.

By the time the foursome made it to the prom, all the embarrassment and pain from the earlier incident had dissipated. Inside the hall, a lot of people stopped to stare at Michelle. She was beautiful, there was no doubt about it, but she didn't seem to notice their attention. Instead, she asked Karrie to give her the rundown on all the cliques, who was cool and who was not.

"I don't know who's cool," Karrie said as they approached the punch bowl. "I only know that I am not."

"Ridiculous girl." Michelle handed Karrie a cup full of punch. "You're the coolest person in this room."

"Are your being incongruent in your definition of coolness?" Karrie took a sip of punch.

"No, I'd say anyone who cannot see your coolness is incongruent in their reasoning and *their* definition of coolness."

"I can tell you one person everyone thinks is cool," Karrie whispered, pointing at a guy across the room. "His name is Richard, and he is definitely cool. And he seems to be looking at you."

"But you don't approve?" Michelle raised her eyebrows as she took a drink.

"I don't know. He's alright, I guess. Everyone else goes out of their way to impress him."

"Not so impressive to me."

"Why?" Karrie asked. "He seems to be taken by you."

"Do you see the beautiful girl next to him? That's his date, I assume."

"Yes, she's also one of the most popular kids in the school."

"But he's looking at me and has his back turned to his girlfriend. Not cool. In fact, tacky and wrong. It is incongruent for him to have a cool reputation." Michelle turned her back to Richard. "What don't you like about him?"

"He picks on Tom and Scott."

"Scott. That nice kid with Down syndrome at punch bowl?"

"Yeah. He imitates him and teases him. He's done it since we were in elementary school."

Michelle rolled her eyes. "What does he mock Tom about?"

"Tom likes poetry and quotes history and stuff like that. That's considered weird around here."

"So, Tom has a brain and Richard doesn't. Tom's intelligence threatens him." Michelle took another sip.

"Quiet. He's coming this way," Karrie whispered.

"Hey, beauties." Richard wiggled his way between the girls. "I think I must be at a model shoot with you two standing here."

"Never noticed me before," Karrie whispered as she turned her back to put her cup on the table.

"Oh dear!" Michelle said in a thick fake Russian accent. "I am not good at your English. You must speak slower. Beauties... it means?"

"Uh... I don't know," Richard stammered. "It means you look good."

"Is it the custom for us to return such a nice saying?"

"I guess." Richard looked helpless.

"I don't know what to say." Michelle looked at fingers nails and she smiled. "You left a beautiful woman to compliment two other women in front of her. It is unseemly behavior to me."

"She can take care of herself," Richard mumbled.

"But should she if she is with you?" Michelle looked directly into his eyes. "This is unseemly to me."

There was an awkward moment of silence when Richard looked at Michelle.

"Now we have music. You must go back to your date, and this time," Michelle slowed her speech and over-enunciated each word. "Be kind to her." Michelle walked over to the punch bowl and stood by Scott.

A slight whisper of 'b-u-r-r-r-n' rippled across the crowd.

"No private conversations here, I guess," Karrie laughed, pouring herself another drink. The microphone squeaked, and Ms. Write stood on the stage. "We usually have a dance-off between two school clubs to open the festivities."

"Maybe not this time!" Tom shouted from the back of the room.

Richard walked up to the stage with his date. "Let's have a dance-off between the nerds and the cool kids."

"I think we are far too enlightened and sophisticated to identify some students as nerds and others as cool," Mrs. Write said.

"No, we're not." Tom smiled at Richard. "I'll take your challenge. We don't have to waste time identifying the nerds and who's cool." He put his arm around the date, Katrina. She was on the cheer team and arguably the best dancer in the school, but she stiffened and pulled away.

"It's okay," Richard smirked at Katrina. "I can win this thing on my own. I chose a classic. "Uptown Funk."

"Okay," Tom shrugged his shoulders. "We'll go with…"

"The Hokey Pokey!" Scott blurted out from the back of the room.

Laughter scattered across the room and Tom tried to change the song by suggesting different titles, 'or we could try "Dance, Dance," "We are Young," and "Titanium," but the kids started chanting, "Hokey Pokey! Hokey Pokey!" He nodded his head and looked at the lead singer.

The leader of the band nodded. Two of the background singers put their mouths to the microphone and blew out a rapid rhythm, then the lead singer started to rap.

"Hey there, peeps, we're going to play a game.

We're not immature. We're merely insane.

You put your right foot in and take it out.

Don't lift your snout, 'cause it's the Hokey Pokey,

and it's what it is all about."

The electric guitar screeched, and everyone rushed to the dance floor. The singer rapped the coolest version of "The Hokey Pokey" that Karrie had ever heard. The room flooded with laughter as the band called out new moves to the dance. When the band transitioned to "Uptown Funk," the last few stragglers ran onto the floor to join the dance. Amidst the laughter and the adrenalin, everyone forgot about the contest.

Karrie, Josh, Scott, Tom, and Michelle formed a tight circle where they could all dance and mirror each other's moves. Karrie knew they would be teased again on Monday and left to eat lunch in the corner behind the library. Richard would move back to the top of the pecking order and mock the way Scott walked and Tom's historical quotes, but that was Monday, which seemed so far away. Tonight, they were stars, and it was beautiful. Somehow, they had won, and the victory felt sweet.

Karrie's heart melted when Josh's parents met them in the parking lot and announced a cruise around San Diego's harbor. She had never been on a boat, though she had watched them all her life while living in downtown San Diego. She often wondered what it would be like to glide from Coronado Island to the front street. It seemed like a dream when she stepped onto the Dalman's sailboat.

The night whispered promises of happily ever after.

"Best day ever." Karrie snuggled up to Tom.

"How it ends is more important than how it begins," Michelle laughed from the front of the boat.

Karrie relaxed with each wave that lapped against the boat's side. Home seemed as far away as Monday. She closed her eyes and tried to pretend that Mr. and Mrs. Dalman were her parents.

Almost as if Tom could hear her thoughts, he whispered, "You know, it doesn't bother me."

"What doesn't bother you?" She lifted her head from his shoulder.

"What happened tonight."

"You mean at the prom?"

"No, at your house with your mom and your neighborhood."

Karrie saw Michelle turn around and glare at Tom.

"It was a mistake. My mom didn't do anything wrong."

"I know. What I meant to say was the situation doesn't bother me. You know, about where you come from and where you live."

"What's wrong with where I live?"

Out of the corner of her eye, she saw Josh wave his arms.

Tom fumbled his words. "I just wanted to make this vow—this promise to you tonight—that I would never make you feel less… than anyone else."

"Tom, you're boring everyone with your archaic medieval bigotry." Michelle glared at Tom.

Karrie went numb as Tom tried to take back his words. Michelle made a joke to break the tension, but Karrie didn't laugh. Tom's failed speech made her feel ashamed. Even Michelle's and Josh's supportive looks increased the shame. She thought the joy of the evening had outshone the evening's painful beginning, but it had not. The victory she had enjoyed melted away. She forced a smile and whispered, "It's okay. You can tell me when you find better words to describe what you're feeling." She pressed her lips up against Tom's. Tom closed his eyes but did not return her kiss.

"Let's just listen to the water." She rested her head uneasily on Tom's shoulder.

Chapter Eight

Something That Won't Stay Buried

Daniel's Funeral

Lo'laini's Greif, Sandra Struggle.

Lo'laini snuck out her phone to text Karrie while Tutu bowed her head in prayer.

<Where U@?>

<On the balcony, I can see u with your aunts. In the front pew>

<can you come down here?>

<We tried, there's too many people.>

<We? Who u with>

< Tom and Josh, ya said you didn't mind, right?>

<Yeah, but now I just want a see ya, feeling so alone>

< usher keeps directing us upstairs, we'll try to push our way thru.>

< please, push your way thru.>

"Lo'laini?"

She looked up to see Tutu frowning at her.

"Put your phone away. This is no time to text. You must be here with your family."

"It hurts too much to be here, Tutu."

"Escaping into your phone won't take away the pain. It will just delay it. It's better to feel the pain when you are with the people you love, your family." Tutu put her arm around Lo'laini.

Lo'laini rested her head against her grandmother's neck while warm tears spilled down her cheeks. She turned and saw Aunt Emily smiling at her while Aunt Sandra sat with her arms crossed.

"It'll be over soon," Aunt Emily said as she passed Karrie a mint.

"Not soon enough," Aunt Sandra whispered.

At the front of the church, Pastor Mike stood to one side of the cross with his head bowed in prayer. A guitarist strummed a mixture of songs. When the last melody ended, he started to walk off stage but stopped and asked Pastor Mike, "Can I say something?"

"Of course." Mike motioned him to the podium.

The guitarist cleared his voice and rested, shaking hands on the podium. "Some of you know Daniel and I were good friends. We went to the same A.A. meeting."

Aunt Sandra tapped her fingers on the red-cushioned pew.

"My name is Ken, and I'm an alcoholic."

"Hi, Ken." Some of the congregation automatically chanted, then embarrassed laughter rippled across the congregation.

"We're not at a meeting, but old habits die hard." Ken wiped his eyes. "Here in this sanctuary, we don't just have a higher power. We have a Lord, who is Jesus."

Ken's look caught Lo'laini's eye. "Daniel loved you and your mother so much. He also loved the Lord, but he had an anguish inside him that started when he was a kid. It was a tender spot that tormented him and made him vulnerable. Sometimes, when that torment intensified, he reached for the booze. Then, after he found his faith, he sobered up for twelve years. When you were just a little one, I visited your house, and life seemed so clean and fresh. But alcoholism is a cunning and baffling disease and he started to use it again after your mom died."

Ken wiped his eyes again and pulled a Bible out from under the podium. "I've been thinking about a verse Pastor Mike shared with me when I tried to understand Daniel's death. In second Samuel fourteen, verse fourteen, it says, "Like water spilled on the ground, which cannot be recovered, so we must die. But God does not take away life; instead, he devises ways so that a wandering person may not remain estranged from Him." The first part of that verse means that we're all going die someday." Ken smiled at everyone. "Sorry to deliver that news if you already didn't know it."

Laughter once again rippled across the congregation.

"Have you ever tried to hang on to the water with your hands? Like when you were a kid in a bathtub, did you ever try grabbing water only to have it slip between your fingers? That's what it's like trying to hang on to someone who is suffering from an addiction. No matter how hard you hang on, they can still slip through your fingers. Watching someone you love die from addiction is like trying to grasp water."

Lo'laini noticed the intense look on Sandra's face when Ken talked about trying to grasp water.

"The second part of the verse is more important because it says God does not take away life but provides a way for the wanderer to be at home. What I'm trying to say is the booze made Daniel a stranger on this earth. In the end, he was a wanderer who had a hard time feeling at home on this earth, but now he's with Jesus, and he's finally home. I'm not trying to make excuses for him. I just wanted you to know that Daniel knew Jesus." Ken's voice cracked as he started to cry. "Now he's home with Jesus. He's not wandering anymore."

Pastor Mike placed his hand on Ken's shoulder. Ken turned around and gave Mike a fist bump before walking off the platform.

Mike rested his Bible on the podium and pulled out some notes. "I don't think these are going to do me any good now. Ken, dude, you stole my thunder."

The congregation laughed again.

"I don't think I can add anything more except to quote his daughter, Lo'laini. In regard to Daniel's sobriety, she said he tried. He really tried, but in the end, he got weak. I don't have all the answers here, but in ministry, I've seen addiction take down a lot of good people. Ken quoted the big book of Alcoholic Anonymous when he said alcoholism is a cunning and baffling disease, but I'm a Bible guy. Daniel's struggle reminds me of another scripture. "For now, we see only a reflection as in a mirror; then we shall see face to face. Now I know in part; then I shall know fully, even as I am fully known." This verse is at the end of first Corinthians chapter thirteen, which Christians call the "love chapter." It tells us there are things we don't understand in life, like how one Christian can overcome addiction and one does not, but the Bible also tells us the one thing we can always depend on is love. Paul says at the end of that chapter, "And now these three remain: faith, hope and love. But the greatest of these is love." As we remember Daniel today, we remember him with love, allowing him the same grace to cover his weaknesses that God affords us. We ask for God's mercy to help us with the things we can't see clearly about him."

Pastor Mike looked at Sandra; Sandra quickly looked down and wiped away a tear. "How many of you guys remember the song "Turn, Turn, Turn" by The Byrds?"

A couple of people nodded.

"I like that song," Pastor Mike said. "The lyrics were taken from Ecclesiastes three, verses one through nine. It talks about the turning seasons of life and how each season provides us with what we need for life's tasks, such as building up, tearing down, laughing, grieving, being born, and even dying. The lyrics are literally the first nine verses of Ecclesiastes three. Songs like that make the scriptures come alive! I've got to say the only thing that bothers me about this song is that it stops at the most important verse in the chapter. Verse eleven says, "that God has made everything beautiful in its time." Think about that for a moment. We each have time to be beautiful on this earth. God made Daniel beautiful in his time in his athleticism, love for his daughter, and love for his wife and his sarcastic and quirky sense of humor. Even in his valiant struggle against addiction, God made Daniel uniquely beautiful."

Lo'laini smiled and nodded her head.

"The second part of that verse says, "He has also set eternity in the human heart; yet no one can fathom what God has done from beginning to end. This scripture describes our expectations for eternal life. It's set in our hearts. It's a part of our design." We expect people to live forever. We yearn for it. That's why we feel a sense of emptiness and betrayal when someone we know, who has been a part of our lives, leaves us. The fact that death stuns us is a silent witness that death wasn't a part of God's original plan life. It's hard to accept that Daniel is dead, perhaps because death has not completely swallowed him up. There is a part of Daniel that is still alive. Jesus said, "I am the way and the truth and the life. No one comes to the Father except through me." When Paul spoke about heaven, he said, "For we know that if the earthly tent we live in is destroyed, we have a building from God, an eternal house in heaven, not built by human hands. Meanwhile we groan, longing to be clothed instead with our heavenly dwelling, because when we are clothed, we will not be found naked. For while we are in this tent, we groan and are burdened, because we do not wish to be unclothed but to be clothed instead with our heavenly dwelling so that what is mortal may be swallowed up by life.""

Why does Paul call our human bodies tents? The Jewish faith celebrates their journey in the desert when they fled the slavery of Pharaoh and lived in tents. They understood that their dwellings were temporary. At first, the tents were adequate shelter. They provided shade during the day and warmth at night. But after a while, they began to sag and tear, and the Israelites yearned for something more permeant. You know how things always get broken and lost while you're traveling? Tent living was okay for a short time, but they wanted to settle. They wanted their promised land. They wanted a home.

"The Greek word Paul used for their tent is not only means tent, but a rented tent. In fact, it was the term used for the rent money a person paid for a tent because they did not want to buy it. It is hard to be at rest in a temporary shelter. Maybe that is why this "rented tent" here on earth never feels like home. We don't know what's around the next corner. Paul says that while we're in this tent, we groan. The word he uses also means to sigh. It's a sigh of weariness. I think it's the kind of weariness Ken was talking about. Daniel often felt like a stranger in his struggle against addiction. Now we know he's free from that struggle and at home because all of his groans have been comforted. In your bulletin is the twenty-third, Psalm. We read that at funerals because it describes a journey that ultimately leads home. A journey to rest in God's home. Psalms twenty-three starts with, "The Lord is my shepherd." **The Lord** is a formal name for God. As the Psalm continues, the Lord gets closer to David. He describes God as "**he** makes me lie down in green pastures, **he** leads me beside quiet waters, **he** restores my soul. **He** guides me in paths of righteousness for **his** name's sake." As David continues this journey, God transitions from **he** to **you**. "Even though I walk through the valley of the shadow of death, I will fear no evil, for *You* are with me." You are with me, the Psalmist says. God is with you when you pass through the shadowy place of death."

Pastor Mike looked directly at Aninki, cuddling Lo'laini. "We are in conversation with God when we witness death, and let me tell you, it is not always a polite conversation."

He glanced at Sandra, who was looking at a children's bible she had found in the pew. "But no matter how impolite the conversation may seem, keep it going. In that conversation lies your salvation. Listen to how God comforts us after we pass through the shadowy place. "Your rod and Your staff, they comfort me. You prepare a table before me in the presence of my enemies. You anoint my head with oil, my cup overflows. Surely goodness and love will follow me all the days of my life, and I will dwell in the house of the Lord forever." It's only in the presence of Jesus Christ that any of us can find our true home and our true rest. As a minister of the gospel of Jesus Christ, it is my privilege to tell you that Daniel has found true rest today in his heavenly home and wanders no more."

"Amen," Lo'laini whispered.

"Hallelujah." Aninki squeezed her. Emily placed an arm around Lo'laini and Aninki.

Sandra swallowed hard but didn't look up. "Right, of course," she whispered.

✝

Chapter Nine

Lo'laini's Hearth

Daniel's Repass

At the restaurant, Isabella leaned against the wall by the waitress station, proudly displaying her baby bump. Her smile welcomed Lo'laini after the myriad of faces that had invaded her space at the funeral.

"Your favorite place?" Aninki whispered, pulling Lo'laini close to her.

"Yes, Tutu." Lo'laini smiled at her grandmother.

"We've provided a way for you to be home during this repast." Aunt Emily pointed toward Isabella and Alejandro.

Aunt Sandra placed her hand on Lo'laini's back. "You've been hugged and kissed by too many adults today. It's time for you to be a teenager for a few minutes."

That was true. Before that morning, no person outside Lo'laini's family had ever hugged her. Of course, her old boyfriend Kevin had put his arm around her and kissed her, so had Josh, but Lo'laini made sure the front of her body didn't touch theirs. Lo'laini had only had two boyfriends, and both of them respected her boundaries without her having to say anything. Not even Karrie hugged her, although they sometimes bumped elbows.

But at the funeral, all those adults grabbed her and pressed their bodies to hers, even kissing her on the cheeks. It drove her crazy. Their salvia slickened her cheeks and their perfumes and body odor drenched her. She wanted to scrub herself clean. Lo'laini felt claustrophobic in the crowd ever since her mother died. For the last five hours, a crowd had surrounded her.

Aunt Emily's and Sandra's words relieved her.

Alejandro walked toward her. "Remember a year ago when I told you twenty percent of our profits came from funeral repasts?" He swung out his arm, creating a path through the restaurant.

"Yes, boss."

"It's because we think of things that others do not." Isabella walked over and escorted Lo'laini to the back room.

Isabella opened the door. Karrie, Tom, and Josh sat at a table covered with Lo'laini's favorite foods: rice with kalua pig, pork, and chicken lau lau, pipikaula, and lomi lomi salmon with helpings of poi, and kulolo, and haupia. For dessert, lots of shaved ice.

"My friends," Lo'laini whispered as the four of them formed a huddle. She held up her arms. "No hugging. I've had enough of that today."

"We'll stand and lean against each other for a while then," Josh laughed.

Lo'laini leaned in. It felt good.

"Ok, I'm hungry. Enough of this. To the table!" Tom shouted.

"I know I have what you need most," Karrie said, pulling wet wipes out of a plastic bag.

Lo'laini grabbed the sheet from her hand and wiped her face.

"I saw that avalanche of affection you got after the funeral, and I was wondering how you were managing it," Josh said.

"Not well," Lo'laini said. "Please tell me Miguel did not make this food." She looked at Karrie.

"No," Isabella said. "We fired him. I wish you girls would have told me how he was behaving. I would have fired him earlier."

"But it doesn't matter now." Alejandro nudged his wife. "Now is the time for love, laughter, and kindness between friends."

"You think she can get it from this crew?" Tom laughed.

"It's best that we could do," Alejandro said as he and Isabella turned to leave.

The four friends sat at the table.

"Hey, Lo'laini," Tom said, pointing at her cast. "I know you love bracelets, but I think that white one is carrying it a bit too far."

The group laughed.

"Thanks," Lo'laini said. "I knew you would know exactly what to say."

"Seriously, Lo'laini. How are you feeling?" Karrie asked.

"I can't find the words right now." She used her fingers to scoop out two fingers full of poi and lifted it to her lips. When she saw the look of horror on Josh's and Tom's faces, she said, "That's how it's done, dudes. If you don't like it, try something else."

Lo'laini and Karrie nudged each other.

Tom started to dip his fingers in the poi when Lo'laini said, "Okay, you don't have to eat it the way that I do. You can use a spoon. Better yet, use a piece of spicy pork. Most tourists don't like poi because it's bland, but they smile and gulp it down to be polite. I don't want you to do that here."

The group filled their plates with Lo'laini's favorite foods. She smiled to herself. Her best friends were so "white and touristy." She had never noticed it before.

She played with the sticky rice, rolling it up in a small bite size balls. "You asked about my feelings. I kind of feel like a haole."

Confusing looks met her words.

"Haole is a Hawaiian word that means a person without a homeland." Lo'laini could see her friends still did not understand. "When you were a kid and saw a line of ants walking across the concrete, did you ever use your foot or finger to smash some of the ants?"

No one answered.

"Well, I did. I would smash the ones before and behind an ant. That would leave one ant all alone. That ant would frantically run around, trying to find a path because no one was there to show it the way. It's lost, and you can see it by the way it runs around."

Everyone stared at the food in front of them.

"That sounds like a harsh place to be," Josh said.

"I'm sorry, Lo'laini," Karrie said.

They could hear fireworks exploding over the ocean in the room's quietness.

"Sea World fireworks," Tom said. "You know it's summertime in San Diego by them."

Karrie nudged Tom. "Let's go look at the fireworks."

"That sounds like a good idea." Tom got up with Karrie, which left Lo'laini and Josh alone at the table.

Lo'laini rolled more sticky rice into balls.

"Is it okay that I'm here?" Josh asked.

"Yeah. I told Karrie I wanted you to be here. Not as my boyfriend. I can't do that now, you understand?"

Josh nodded.

"Don't get me wrong. I liked the flowers and romance and stuff, but not now. It's not what I liked the most about our friendship anyway." Lo'laini's voice trembled, and a warm tear tumbled down her cheek. "It was the conversations, swimming at the beach together, and the walks where nothing particularly romantic happened, but I had fun with you like I was still a kid."

"Since Mom died and when I was put in foster care, I stopped feeling like a kid. The only place I could let my guard down and be a kid was with you, Karrie, and annoying Tom. Our friendship has been an island of normalcy in the middle of all my chaos. Everything has been so crazy these last few years that I never felt like I had time to catch my breath. I always had to be on my guard. Even the adults didn't act like adults, trying to compete over me. Even at school, where I tried to be so cool, I felt as if I could be weird with you guys. Sometimes you've just got to be weird, like Tom, I guess. I could be a kid with you."

Josh shrugged. "It's been a privilege to welcome you to that land of weirdom. Don't worry about Tom. He's weird, but he's a good guy."

"I don't worry about him. I worry about Karrie. He's paper thin, and paper-thin people leave deep cuts." Lo'laini sighed and looked out the window at Karrie and Tom, arm in arm, watching the fireworks. "I hate saying goodbye to you guys." She squeezed Josh's hand. "I want to have romance again, but not until I'm settled. Romance feels more like pretending and I want to work on real stuff. Making a home with my aunts is real, so I don't have time to pretend right now. Do you understand?"

"Yeah."

"No romance means no long-distance friendships. I had that with mom in the hospital with the cancer and then with Dad when he started to use drugs again. I've said too many goodbyes with the expectation of seeing someone again, only to be disappointed. After tonight we…"

"After tonight, we let it phase out."

"Yeah. In foster care and the restaurant, I'd hear about girls who had similar troubles as me. They felt trapped, as if nothing would ever get better. They didn't have a family, so they would try to make one. They looked for boyfriends to rescue them like knights in shining armor—only they turned out to be just like the guys who abused or abandoned or neglected them." She wiped away a tear.

"It hasn't been that way with you. I've only had two boyfriends, and both of you have been more friends than anything else. I love that because it could have been bad. Instead, it's been good. Thank you, Josh."

"I am glad I could be your friend, Lo'laini."

She rested her head on Josh's shoulder.

"Do you want to join those two ruffians and watch the fireworks?" he asked.

"Yeah."

The sea wind blasted them as they stepped out of the restaurant. Bursts of red, blue, yellow, and pink splashed across the sky, reflecting off Karrie's, Tom's, and Josh's faces. It reminded Lo'laini of the multi-colored haloes in the William Morris-stained glass windows at the All-Saints Church in Sleepy Hollow that Aunt Emily had shown her on her phone yesterday.

"How could something as destructive as dynamite create something so beautiful?" Karrie asked, looking up at the sky.

"Hey, Karrie," Lo'laini said. "Do you want to go scream at the ocean?"

"Scream at the ocean?" Tom asked. "What did the ocean ever do to you?"

"Nothing," Karrie said. "But Lo'laini and I used to scream at it on our late-night shifts while waiting for her dad to pick us up."

Lo'laini kicked off her shoes. "The ocean would roar at us, so we screamed back." She ran toward the ocean, followed by Karrie, Tom, and Josh.

The four teens stood on the windy shoreline. The white waves glowed against the crisp night sky. The ocean's gentle roar encompassed them.

First, Karrie opened her mouth and let out the loudest scream she could. Josh and Tom followed. Lo'laini opened her mouth, but nothing came out. She tried again, only in silence.

Then, from the bottom of her feet, a primeval scream rose inside her. It wasn't just a scream; it was a wail of grief. It was a scream for Queen Liliuokalani's lost kingdom of Hawaii. It was the mournful cry of her grandmother's lost love. It was the grief for her mother's early death and her father's inability to pull himself out of addiction. It was a shout for her lost Hawaiian culture and a cry for a homeland that always seemed to elude her.

Lo'laini gave voice to all muffled screams in her life, and she screamed until she fell to her knees in sobs. When she opened her eyes, her friends surrounded her as if they were huddled in prayer. White foam wrapped its wet arms around them, gently pulling them all out to sea.

"I guess the ocean won this time," Lo'laini said through her sobs.

All four friends sat in silence beneath the star-filled sky and gentle sound of the ocean lapping at their feet.

Chapter Ten

Karrie's New Foundation

<From: Karriebear > <To: Lunigirl >

Hey Lo'laini,

Sorry it's taken me so long to email you. I wanted to talk to you so badly during the funeral. Especially after you cried at the ocean. Remember how all the adults came out and surrounded you! I couldn't push through. It seemed like I was trying to push through all day. Are you sure you're, okay? Your aunts seemed nice, but England??!!! That's too far away!!! What am I going to do without you girl!!!

Josh says hi. He went to Bible college with Tom. I saw him at the restaurant before he left. It was awkward. I think I reminded him of you. I believe he liked you more than he let on.

Isabella's on leave. She's been worried about her mom, whose cancer has been complicated by dementia, so she hasn't been at the restaurant

lately. Did I tell you she asked me to live in the little house behind home?
Weird, uh?

As I said, Tom's away at Bible college. He left Tuesday, but I think
he left long before that. He hung out with me, but he wasn't really there
with me. Something changed, and I can't figure it out.

I miss you, girl. I miss you so much! I could use some advice. I
registered for San Diego City College classes—only because Isabella
bugged me so much about it. But Mom doesn't like me being there. She
thinks it's a waste of time. She encouraged me to find a vocational track
and not think about a four-year degree. But I love college. I like reading,
writing and even lectures. This semester I'm taking world history,
philosophy, and freshman English. The restaurant is a lonely place
without you.

Hope things are good for you in the U.K. Write soon.
Karrie>

Karrie looked up from her phone as the bus pulled up to
San Diego City College. Karrie glanced at the time: 9 a.m. If
she hurried, she could get to her class in fifteen minutes. She'd
be late, but at least she's made it.

After she rushed across campus, the wooden door creaked
as she pulled it open, then tiptoed into class. She blushed when
several students looked at her. Soon the professor's lecture
captured her attention. Stories about the great Roman culture
crumbling inside their fortified walls while noble scholars
watched their illiterate barbarian conquers in puzzlement.

"What were the two most significant historical trends in the Middle Ages?" Dr. Downs asked, looking across the classroom.

Karrie timidly raised her hand.

"Yes." He checked his seating chart. "Ms. O'Leary."

"The rise of the convent and monastery systems and the decline of an educated population due to the plagues from the vast amount of travel due to the Crusades."

"Exactly. For those of you who did not read your text, one of the myriad causes of the plagues was infected fleas on rats that traveled from warships used during the Crusades, but not all was lost. Out of that great depression of the Middle Ages came the Reformation and the Enlightenment."

"It must be great to be the smartest girl in the class," whispered a male voice behind Karrie.

"It would be if there were any girls in the class, but since no one here is under the age of twelve, you must be referring to women," whispered a female seated next to her.

"I hate to invade your social calendars." Dr. Downs's voice caught Karrie's attention again. "But the next three chapters are due next week. Class dismissed."

Karrie turned to get her backpack. A beaming blonde-haired guy leaned back in his chair, looking up at her. Standing beside him was an older woman carrying her books on her hip as if they were a young child.

"You got no choice," the guy said. "You must join us for our breakfast bull session."

Karrie reached into her pocket and fumbled for money. She had enough for coffee, a donut, and bus fare. "What's a bull session?"

"It's a poor excuse for a study group, and we need you," the older woman said. "I'm Laura, and this smart mouth is Keith. Don't worry about the cost. I got you today."

Karrie blushed as she swung her backpack over her shoulder. They walked toward the door.

"Ms. O'Leary, can you visit me during office hours today?"

"Ow. You're in trouble," Keith whispered in a sing-song voice as he opened the door.

"More likely, she'll be commended for being the most prepared in class today." Laura took Karrie's arm. "Be honest, Karrie. Have you had any breakfast this morning?"

"I grabbed some coffee before I got on the bus this morning."

"Then I think eggs, bacon, and hash browns won't be unwelcome."

Karrie blushed and nodded.

At the cafeteria, she found a table near a window in the front while Keith and Laura got in line. Karrie rested her chin on her hand as she gazed at the students sauntering across the campus.

It seemed like a miracle for her to be in college after all the trouble she had experienced in school. Besides the constant bullying and always being in the slowest reading group in school, she also had to deal with sleepless nights because of the violence at home so she wasn't prepared for college. Even though she loved learning, she never could concentrate on school tasks and never got good grades.

In the middle school while she was living in a group home, she learned to keep her head down and not to draw attention to herself. She never raised her hand in class like she did that morning. That was new. The voice of confidence was growing inside her, piercing through the darkness of the past. It was a sophisticated voice, and people listened to it. It felt good.

"Bacon, eggs, hash browns. I hope it's all to your liking." Laura set a plate before her.

"Thanks." Karrie poked the yoke and the soft yellow center spilled into her crispy hash browns. She salted them and scooped up the perfect bite.

"A breakfast connoisseur." Keith laughed as he bit into his breakfast burrito.

"To business." Laura opened her notebook.

"No." Keith blurted around a mouth full of food. "Breakfast and conversation first. That's what separates us from animals, you know. So, Karrie, who are you? Why are you here? And most important of all, do you have a boyfriend?" He rested his chin on his hand.

"Oh, Keith," Laura groaned.

He laughed, "I've got nothing to be ashamed of. I'm just asking for pertinent information."

"No, you're asking an impertinent question."

"I think I would rather find out who you guys are before giving out any information," Karrie said shyly.

"That's not a bad idea." Laura put her notebook away. "Let's start with building a little trust. I'm Laura, much older than both of you. I'm married with two kids in middle school and have returned to school to get a teaching degree. At forty, that might be a long shot or a folly, but here I am, and I'm pretty lucky to have a husband who supports me in this endeavor."

"My turn. I'm Keith. I'm at a junior college because my cheap parents said I could complete my general education here and then apply to university. I'm doing okay in this class. I met Laura in the library and discovered we did better when we created a timeline that traces world events and the prevalent philosophy of the age."

"Can I see it?" Karrie asked.

Laura pulled a large, taped-together sheet of paper out of her notebook. Karrie leaned over to examine it.

"Amateurs." Keith pulled out his laptop. "I saved mine on an Excel sheet."

"I'm not sophisticated enough to use a computer that well, so I stick to paper. This timeline really works for me."

"It worked for both of us," Keith said. "We got perfect scores on the last exam."

Karrie gasped, "I didn't. This timeline is so cool. Can you tell me how you used it to study?"

"No way, at least not until you tell us something about yourself. You're not avoiding the task you forced us to do, are you? Let's see some vulnerabilities. Your turn to talk," Keith said.

"I'm Karrie. I'm in school. I was thinking about getting an A.A., then working on a bachelors, but Mom thinks I should switch to a vocational track because she thinks my current track isn't going to lead anywhere. I don't know anymore." Karrie stirred her hash browns again. "I'm not very good at this stuff. I have to work really hard to get passing grades."

"That doesn't make any sense. You always know what you're talking about in class." Keith closed his computer.

"I've got dyslexia, so..."

"A classic symptom of dyslexia is verbal ability exceeding written ability," Laura said. "My youngest has it. A school psychologist diagnosed her in the sixth grade. Have you registered with the Disabled Student Union? They have services you could use."

Having taken her last bite, Karrie pushed her plate away. "I know I should. I don't know what's stopping me. On a lighter point, I have a boyfriend, but he's away at bible college."

"Men are nothing trouble anyway," Keith said. "Karrie, you like school, don't you?"

"I love it," she said.

"Then who cares what your mom says? The vocational track is great for people who don't want the four-year track, but you should go for it if you want it." Keith moved closer to Karrie.

"It can be a lot of money. I was in foster care, so they'll pay my tuition if I go to school fulltime, but I can't do that because I still have living expenses." Karrie watched students pass by the window.

"You have a lot of decisions to make." Laura reached over and squeezed Karrie's hand.

"But not now." Karrie glanced at the clock. "I've got to get to Dr. Downs's office." She picked up her backpack and slung it over her shoulder. "Do we meet here every Tuesday after class?"

"Yup." Keith pulled out his phone. "Let me have your email, and I'll send you the timeline with instructions about how we're using it in the class."

"Karriebear@gmail.com," Karrie said over her shoulder as she walked out of the room and toward the faculty offices. Dr. Downs's door was open, so she knocked on the door frame.

"Come in and take a seat, Ms. O'Leary," Dr. Downs said, looking over his glasses. He put aside the stack of papers he was grading.

"What's that smell?" Karrie asked as she sat in a chair.

"Liverwurst and onions with hot mustard. Want some?" He held up a paper bag from under his desk.

"No, I just had breakfast. Do you like that stuff?"

"I hate liverwurst, especially with hot mustard, but my in-laws think I like it. When I was courting my wife eons ago, I made the mistake of complimenting my future mother-in-law's liverwurst sandwich. I didn't like it, but I was trying to impress them with my good manners. We've been married for thirty-five years now, and every time my in-laws visit, my mother-in-law brings me a liverwurst sandwich. She's so proud of it that I've never had the heart to tell her I hate it, so I dutifully eat them. That's something I was taught in childhood: waste not, want not." He dropped the bag in his briefcase. "I'll save it for later."

He went back to his pile of papers. "Let me see if I can find your last essay. You have an excellent philosophical grasp of the content, and your writing is beautiful, except for the mechanics. I suspect a learning disability of some sort?"

"Dyslexia." Karrie blushed.

"Dyslexia is nothing about which to be embarrassed. We have an excellent Disabled Student Union here. Register with them. They can enlist a tutor to help you. After that, I expect to see your educational career soar."

"I don't know. I'm thinking about changing to the vocation track anyway. Maybe culinary arts."

"Still, register with the student union. Written communication is important in the professional world as well. You'll need to master these mechanics if you change to the vocational tract too. So, what inspired your desire to transfer?" Downs said without looking up from Karrie's essay.

"I had a fight with my mom this morning. It was a real scream out, but I kind of got what she was trying to say. She doesn't think I'm college material. You can see that I am not particularly good at this stuff. Every paper I get back is marked up with red dots."

"That's mechanics, academics is more than mechanics. You understand philosophy very well and you can intuitively explain it. You do have to find ways to compensate for your disability, and that needs to happen whether you study carpentry, cosmetology, business management, marketing, or philosophy. So, tell me about this fight with your mom."

"Money is short. She said she can't wait four years for me to contribute to the household income. She said it's not going to come to anything anyway. What am I going to do with all this education?"

"Lecture, write, teach, speak, think. Teach others to teach, write, and think. The possibilities are endless." Dr. Downs put down Karrie's essay, leaned forward, and asked, "How old is your mother, Karrie?"

"What does my mom's age have to do with anything?"

"For a woman to have a child your age, she must be an adult. I am guessing you're around eighteen or nineteen."

"I'm eighteen."

"Okay, that means your mom was capable of getting pregnant eighteen years ago, so I am assuming that she is not so old and frail that she needs someone to take care of her. She must be over the age of consent. My point is that your mom's an adult and capable of taking care of herself."

Dr. Downs took off his glasses and rubbed his eyes. "Look, Karrie. I'm an instructor at a junior college who's five years away from retirement. I'm not a particularly wise sage, but I've spent most of my life trying to get bored students to understand how ancient thought has any relevance to their lives, but occasionally, a student comes along whose eyes light up when they make the connection. You're one of those students. For a lot of students, the vocational track is a viable option that can provide a stable job with a decent salary in a few years. Not everyone needs higher education, but some people yearn for it. You seem like someone who yearns for it. Do you like the culinary arts?"

Karrie shook her head. "It was my mom's suggestion. I get what you're saying. It's just that I have other obligations."

"I grew up with a single mom too. I know what poverty feels like. I know how it feels when you think all the good things in life were reserved for richer people."

"That's exactly how I feel. Like I'm sitting at this banquet table full of delicious food, but it's in the middle of the table, so I can't reach it. I can see it, smell it, and I long for it, but I can never reach it."

Dr. Downs smiled, "Explained like a true philosopher. That is very well put. I was the first in my family to attend college and get a doctorate. I heard my fair share of arguments over my education had nothing to do with the real world. My mom could not contribute to my education either. But she also didn't expect me to support her."

"I do have to contribute."

"I did too, but there's a difference between giving your mom some money to help with household expenses and being told to put off your education to support her."

"I guess it would be easier to defend the educational costs if I knew what I would do after graduating." Karrie looked down at her hands.

"You don't have to defend your educational plans to anyone but yourself. Besides, most freshmen don't know their career choice when they enter college. The first years of college are supposed to help you figure that out." He looked down at Karrie's essay again. "I was pretty impressed with your paper on Platonism and Jesus's Sermon on the Mount. Have you thought of a career in theology?"

"I don't believe that women can teach or preach. I mean to say that I was raised to believe that women can't be theologians because they're not allowed to teach or preach to men."

"No, Ms. O'Leary. I think you meant to say you were raised to believe that women shouldn't teach or preach, so they shouldn't be theologians. You made a grammatical error. Shouldn't is not the same as can't. By using the modal verb *can't* between women and theologians, you were saying it would be physically impossible for women to understand and communicate theology."

"Women can become ministers and theologians. It happens all the time. There is nothing in their biological makeup that forbids them from becoming clergy. What you meant to communicate is that someone taught you that women were forbidden to teach or preach, thus, they were discouraged from seeking a theological career. You made a grammatical error, and if you don't mind me saying it, I think that could be a philosophical error as well. You might want to take the time to study alternate opinions on what Scripture has to say about that subject. Did you mean to say that your church doesn't ordain women?"

"I was taught that women shouldn't teach or preach, but my current church does ordain women. We have a female pastor on staff, but I've never talked to her. I guess I don't believe that women should be ordained. I can't prepare for a vocation that I don't believe that I can fulfill. It would be a waste of money."

"That's a strong statement. As a budding young philosopher, you might want to discuss that thesis with that female minister."

Karrie shrugged.

"At any rate, you don't have to decide on your track until the end of the semester. Register with the Disabled Student Union, get a tutor, and consider your options."

Karrie forced a smile.

"One more thing, Ms. O'Leary. Remember that your mother is an adult and can take care of herself. Your job is to speak for yourself. If you don't acquire that skill, you might spend the rest of your life eating liverwurst sandwiches." Dr. Downs smiled and Karrie laughed.

†

Chapter Eleven

The Comfort of Familiarity: Lo'laini's Journey

"You two look drenched to the bone! What happened?" Emily jumped up from the sofa and ran toward Lo'laini and Sandra, who stood outside, wiping their feet on the mat.

"We got caught in the downfall," Lo'laini said as she stomped her muddy feet, loosening the last piece of earth off the soles of her boots.

"It's quite tipping down out there." Sandra slipped off her scarf and wrung it out on the porch. "Leave the door open for a minute, dear."

"Let's get you beside the fire and take these wet things off, then get you into something warm." Emily grabbed a blanket and wrapped Lo'laini in it as she guided her toward the fire. "I've put the kettle on when I heard you coming toward the door."

While Lo'laini slipped off her trousers and sweater, Sandra took a towel to her hair. "I'll bet you're not used to weather like this."

"We have lots of rain on the islands—Hawaii's a rainforest—but this rain is colder here than at home. It chills rather than refreshes. In California, it only rains for one month out of the year. People go crazy during that month."

"I'll take over here." Emily took the towel from Sandra. "You get into something warm and dry yourself off."

She rubbed Lo'laini's hair more gently than Sandra did. "California's technically a desert, but I don't think that fine weather makes for very solid stock. I've noticed that Californians complain easily." She wrapped a blanket tightly around Lo'laini.

"This blanket is warm." Lo'laini pulled it tighter over bare shoulders.

"I wrapped it around soapstone. I keep them in the fireplace, and when the rocks are red hot, I place them in the folds of my blankets. It's a rather old-fashioned idea, but it works well." Emily handed Lo'laini her pajamas. She slipped them on underneath her blanket while Emily hung her clothing by the fire.

"I think an electric heating pad would work much better at keeping you warm in the winter, but my sister is quite a sentimentalist when it comes to customs." Sandra carried a tray of mugs and a teapot into the room. "Sit down, Emily. I'll serve tea. I also pulled the biscuits out of the oven. Thanks for making them."

"Not a problem. I wanted to give you a proper tea when you got home after your day."

"I'm not used to drinking warm tea," Lo'laini smiled.

Sandra handed her a mug. "We can offer you coffee, cider, or hot cholate if you prefer."

"No, tea is fine." Lo'laini took the mug and settled onto the sofa.

"How was your day?" Emily sat on a pile of warm blankets she kept by the fire.

"Quite well, don't you think, Lo'laini?" Sandra sat in the armchair beside the fire.

"Yes, it was fun. I was impressed with Aunt Sandra's authority. She's the boss of everything around here." Lo'laini took a sip of tea.

"She's a bit of the boss in here as well." Emily took a biscuit from the tray.

"Not the boss. More like the accountant," Sandra said. "People know I keep track of the finances, but I have to decide what makes a profit and what costs too much to keep around. We run Larks Gale Place through a board of trustees." Her phone buzzed. "Another work texts. After this one, I'm going to turn this off and business will be finished for the day."

Emily mouthed *she's the boss* to Lo'laini. When Sandra looked up, Emily asked, "Did you meet Sandra's young man?"

"Emily, you know I don't have a young man. If I did, he wouldn't be young, he'd be as middle-aged as I am." Sandra turned off her phone and dropped it into her pocket.

"She's talking about Michael, the chef at our tea house."

"The Jamaican man? You're, like, his girlfriend?"

"I'm not sure it's proper to describe someone my age as a *girl* anything. You might say he's my significant other if he *was* my significant other, which I don't think he is. And Michael does not only work at our tea shop. He has a chain of restaurants, and he's training some of the staff for the next few weeks. You tasted his jam today, Lo'laini."

"It was delicious!" Lo'laini smiled. "Who would have thought of white chocolate and strawberry jam in one jar?"

Sandra nodded. "We're hoping it will sell. We recently entered a business arrangement where we produce the jam here. If they sell, we'll expand into something more lucrative."

"So, is the relationship going anywhere?" Lo'laini smiled.

"Going anywhere? You are really making too much of this, Lo'laini. Michael and I are in a comfortable stationary relationship. We don't need to go anywhere."

"It's a great jam, but I was more impressed with his pastries when we were in kitchen," Lo'laini said, "He could really use that pastry bag. I wanted to be a chef for a while."

"That could be suitable, but the real money is in management and production. Oh, blast!" Sandra picked up her phone. "I need to make a call." She got up and left the room.

"What about you, Aunt Emily? Do you have someone?"

"I did at one time, but that was before you were born. We were married for six years. Then Desert Storm stole him from me."

"That's the war that messed up my dad," Lo'laini said.

"That's what wars do, don't they? I'm glad God lent him to me for those years, but I don't think I want someone else in my life at this point. I gave my heart away once, and once was enough. Now I have my students and manage this small cottage for Sandra and myself."

"You're not involved in the family business at all, then?"

"No," Emily said, looking into the fire. "Technically, I have a vote at the trustee's meeting, and I receive a stipend from the profits, but that's all. Sandra was modest when she said she was the accountant. Many estates like Larks Gale Place have tried to recreate themselves as recreational venues but failed. Sandra's the driving force behind the success of this great house. She was disappointed your dad didn't take charge of the family business, but she's more suited for the position. I've often wondered if she felt somewhat relieved when he refused to be a part of the business. I don't think she would have inherited her position unless he declined to take it. That's one reason she's so excited that you're here. I think she's hoping you'll take his place, so Daniel's voice can still echo in this household through you, but I have a feeling you'd rather be in the kitchen like Michael."

Lo'laini nodded. "I think so, but I'm not sure yet."

"Please, humor her for now. You're only beginning your stay here. I think she'll recognize your passions and support you in whichever career you choose."

Emily looked at the clock wall. "Look at the time. I've got to get dinner together. I left your laptop on the desk so you can email Karrie before dinner."

"Thanks, Aunt Emily."

Lo'laini got up and took her laptop to the blankets where Aunt Emily had been sitting. She nestled into the pile, which smelled like Aunt Emily's perfume. Aunt Sandra talked on the phone in the back room and pans clattered in the kitchen as Lo'laini wrapped the blankets tighter around her, then opened her laptop.

<From: Lunigirl> <To: Karriebear>

Hey girl,

I miss you too! Sorry about the awkwardness with Josh. I heard about Isabella's mom. I met Agostina once after work. I heard she walked here from Guatemala. I tried to talk to her, but she seemed pretty tight-lipped about everything. There seems to be some hostility between her and Isabella on that subject.

I hate that you feel so alone, but I'm glad school is good. I might be crazy, but moving into Isabella's house doesn't sound like a bad idea to me. Sorry about Tom too, but you know me—I don't think he is that great of a loss. I know you like him, but he is paper thin, girl! Even when he's great to be around, he's shallow. I know we don't agree on this, so I won't say anymore.

Things are good here. I admit that I felt overwhelmed when I first saw Larks Gale Estate, the family estate. The house seems like a cross between a castle and a doll house with pink walls and stained-glass windows. I was relieved when I found out my aunts live in a small cottage in the back. It was the servant's quarters, like a hundred years ago. They've built it on and made it a comfortable cottage.

Aunt Emily makes the house snug and fills it with good smells and soft pillows while Aunt Sandra manages everything. The family's primary business is producing wool, so they have a lot of sheep. But Aunt Sandra expanded the business to include a resort so she could keep Larks Gale estate while still making a profit from wool.

They use the house as a hotel with a tearoom and a small restaurant. They rent some plots of land to farmers, but they also have a golf course, tennis courts, and stables where they rent out horses to ride. There's a garden, and they sell organic fruits along with homemade jams and jellies. Aunt Sandra oversees it all!!

It's so cool to watch her working while everyone around her scrambles to make sure they meet her standards. They all seem to like her too. I'm not used to seeing women in charge in my family. Women are usually the ones running around trying to make things work while men gave the orders. It's good to see it the other way around.

I don't know why my dad hated this place so much. I like it. I miss my tutu. She's coming to visit next spring. It still hurts when I think of mom and dad, but I like it here, at least for now. Tell Isabella I'm praying for her mom.

Love ya, girl. Talk soon.

Luni.

Chapter Twelve

Agostina's Journey: Home

Nogales Mission, Arizona/Mexican Border, 1985

Agostina didn't know how long she had been at the mission. She drifted in and out of sleep. She could hear the voices around her. She wanted to rouse herself from her heavy sleep, but her body would not budge.

"Don't wake up. Let her sleep, little angel. Look at her burned and bruised feet. She's lucky she wasn't attacked by a coyote in that desert."

"Animal or human coyote?"

Through a sleepy squint, Agostina saw a formidable older woman with motherly eyes gazing down at her while speaking to a younger woman at her side.

"Both," the older woman said, wiping Agostina's face with a handkerchief. "How's her little one?"

"Curled up like a cat on a mama's stomach," the younger woman said.

"Best place for a little one to be, near her mama's heart. Make sure she has plenty of blankets."

The older woman left the room. Agostina could hear tambourines and Pentecostal songs. She wiggled her bandaged, blistered toes, now bathed in mediated ointment. Who had been so kind to help her? She could not remember.

Isabella yawned, then heaved a sigh as she drifted further into sleep. A slide show of images played in Agostina's mind; the horrific image of her beloved home in Kano, sacked and burnt; running through the night to get to the train station; the soldiers boarding the train and ordering passengers off; escaping into the canyon during the confusion; the many plantations where she stopped to work for a week or two before traveling on; the cool nights and hot desert days alone with a baby on her journey.

Isabella had grown into a toddler. When she was too big for Agostina to carry on her back, she carried her in a basket. When Isabella outgrew the basket, Agostina found a small cart and pulled her. As Isabella grew, Agostina realized she could no longer make the journey independently. She welcomed the company when she came upon a caravan operated by two coyotes. She didn't need someone to smuggle her into the

United States. She had papers, but she thought it wise not to tell anyone about her status.

They welcomed her on, and she would pay them when she arrived at her destination. The price seemed suspiciously low, but her water had depleted, and she could not continue on alone.

She'd traveled with the small party until they reached Nogals, a city a few miles from the Arizona border. The caravan walked for two weeks, stopping only four hours a night for rest. When their leaders suggested a full night's rest, the promise of eight hours of sleep by a warm fire was a welcomed proposition.

Agostina nestled close to the crackling flames after feeding and washing Isabella in a nearby stream. The pop and crackle of the fire calmed fussy Isabella. A sleepy harmonica played familiar Christmas carols, which the travelers hummed while staring into the brisk night sky. Agostina listened as the songs conjured up images of Christmas celebrations surrounded by loved ones in homes engulfed with the smells of homecooked meals, including tapado--a seafood soup with green plantain slices—chiles rellenos, and bell peppers stuffed with meat and vegetables covered in whipped egg whites.

When Agostina first joined the party, everyone talked disdainfully about Guatemala. They spoke of the great disorder caused by migrating mercenary soldiers and the loss of family and friends. But the farther they traveled toward an unknown future, the more they yearned for home. They spoke wistfully about the pointed green hills crowned with misty clouds and adobe cathedrals in Guatemala.

Two weeks into her journey with them. Agostina started to have second thoughts. She lay by the fire, considering her options. Isabella grew heavy in Agostina's arms, and she lay close to her baby and began to drift off into sleep while listening to the people around her describe their home.

She knew nothing about her brother-in-law, only that her husband once said his brother liked tequila. She knew less about the country he lived in. She never believed the stories of untold wealth in the United States. She had heard of people losing everything traveling to the border only to be swallowed up by the masses of immigrants and never heard of again.

I could still make it home. She knew and understood home. Perhaps she could find a corner in Guatemala where violence and war had not scarred. Overcome with drowsiness, Agostina fell asleep.

In the middle of the night, she became aware that two smugglers stood over her. She kept her eyes closed, pretending to be asleep while holding Isabella tighter. They speculated how much her child might sell for.

Once they were out of sight, she wrapped Isabella in her wool poncho and gathered her pouch of supplies. She grabbed a bottle of lighter fuel left by the fire, poured it on one of the smugglers' sleeping bags, then grabbed a small twig from the fire and lit the bag. It burst into flames. While it burned, she slipped into the canyon as the smugglers cursed, trying to extinguish the fire. Now, she could not turn back. She had to reach the border and create a new life.

She walked for three days, in and out of canyons and off the main road, until she reached the Mexican-Arizona border. She still had most of the money Abisai's brother had sent to him. It would meet her needs for a couple of months in Mexico, but she didn't know how far it would go in the United States. And how would she find her brother-in-law? How would he know her?

She found a hotel and rented a room where she could rest for a night and clean up Isabella. She called her brother-in-law from the lobby three times. The first time, no one picked up. She left a message the other two times, letting him know she would be crossing the border the following day. She described herself because he didn't know what she looked like and the only picture she had of him was taken when he was a teenager.

The following day, Agostina joined the line at the customs office. It wasn't as difficult as she'd anticipated. With her papers in order, they saw nothing suspicious about her visiting her brother-in-law for a couple of months.

But fear set into her gut when she stepped through the gate into Nogales. She scanned the crowd of gaping faces who stared at her in her traditional dress as her daughter danced with her shadow, unaware of the crowd. She walked down the street, gently pulling Isabella's hand. Dazed, she found a bus bench and sat down to ponder her options.

"Lord, what am I going to do now?" She scanned the crowd for a face that resembled her brother-in-law.

Behind her, she heard the familiar tunes of Spanish praise songs. She looked around and saw a store-front church filled with people singing at the top of their lungs. She went across the street, sat in the back of the church, and began to pray. Isabella stood in the aisle and danced to the music. Agostina felt lighter just being inside a church. For the first time in months, she sat among welcoming faces, and she wasn't afraid.

"Welcome," a warm voice said in Spanish behind her. She turned and saw a broad woman with a beaming smile. "I am Maria Morena. You looked tired and a little lost."

"I am both."

"Are you hungry?"

"We've already eaten this morning. I am not poor." Agostina pulled out the envelope with cash.

"Put that away." Maria sat next to Agostina. "How long was your journey?"

"It has felt like many journeys." Her eyes filled with tears.

"Most journeys consist of many journeys." Maria took her hand.

Agostina nodded. "I am supposed to find my brother-in-law, but I don't know what he looks like, and he doesn't know what I look like. May I sit here for your worship service?"

Maria nodded. The music flooded Agostina's tired soul. She lifted her hands and then stood, swaying to the music. Maria stepped to the microphone and began to pray. All the fatigue from the last six months fell onto Agostina. Her knees buckled, and she fell to the ground. She felt hands lifted her as strangers directed her to a back room with a cot.

"I should not stay here," Agostina said.

"Yes, you should. Stay and rest." Maria laid her hand firmly against Agostina's head while placing a warm blanket over her. Isabella crawled onto the cot and cuddled on her mother's stomach. Against her, Agostina fell asleep.

Hours later, she woke to the sound of Isabella's laughter. Agostina's muscles ached as she pulled herself from her cot.

"We didn't want to wake you, so we let you sleep through the night," said a striking young woman with a black braid streaming down her back.

Agostina clutched her cloth bag to her side. The money was still there.

"I'm Letisha. I work with Pastor Maria's mission."

"What a powerful woman." Agostina stood to stretch her arms and legs. "I've never met anyone like her. Who is she?"

"Maria Mornio and you're not the first person to notice her power. She has a great determination to serve the Lord."

"The words she spoke to me keep ringing in my head. One journey takes many journeys." Agostina unraveled her bun and combed her fingers through it until Latisha handed her a brush.

"Maria used to be an advocate for the farm workers' union before she became a preacher. She worked with Cesar Chavez."

"I'm sorry. I know very little about this country."

"Let's just say she made a lot of people's lives better, physically and then spiritually, when God called her to preach."

"Thank you for your kindness," Agostina said. "But I must find a place for my daughter and I to stay. Do you have a phone? I would like to call my brother-in-law and see if he can pick me up here."

"I think he already stopped by," Maria said as she walked into the room. "He was looking for you. He came to the church because he knew you were a praying woman and he hoped he might find you here." She pulled up a chair and sat near Agostina. "How much do you know about your brother-in-law?"

"Not much," Agostina said while gathering her things, calling Isabella to her.

"You didn't have any choice but to flee and to stay with him, even though you don't know him?" Maria asked.

"My husband planned to visit him, but the soldiers…" She started to sob. "I had no choice."

"Too many soldiers," Maria whispered. "How did you protect your little one through all of this?"

Agostina scooped Isabella in her arms. "The best that I could. I do not know my brother-in-law, and I do not know how safe we would be with him without my husband to protect us. But I have a visa, so I am here legally."

"I met him, and he was a bit worse for alcohol." Maria lifted the cot to put it away. "I can get you a list of shelters that are clean and safe and take immigrants. You can stay there while you get to know him before moving in with him."

Agostina nodded again. "Thank you not just for the place to stay but for your kind words. You were corrected yesterday. I have been on many journeys, and my decisions may not have been the wisest decisions."

"But you were never alone, Agostina. With Jesus, you are never alone."

Agostina smiled.

†

Chapter Thirteen

Small Talk over Great Matters

Karrie's Painful Break-up

Watched pots never boil, and a time clock's hands remained stationary in an employee's-tired stare. Karrie had been glancing at the clock since she arrived at eleven a.m. It was her job to chop onions and peppers for the kitchen crew, so she spent her first hour in the refrigerator. She was on the floor waiting at tables by ten. All morning, she watched the clock. Finally, the hour hand inched its way to the four. She motioned to Cindy, another server.

"I hope you enjoyed your meal," Karrie said to her customer. "I'm going off the clock, but Cindy will take care of you for the rest of the evening." Karrie acknowledged the tall thin server next to her. Cindy nodded.

"You've been wonderful," said the middle-aged man at the head of the table. The businesspeople around the table quietly applauded. Karrie blushed and then rushed toward the break room. Cindy followed her.

Since Lo'laini had left over a year ago, Karrie had found a new friend in Cindy, which was a blessing since Tom was still away. They had met at church after Karrie gave her testimony and Cindy started working at the restaurant. Her husband worked in construction and his hours were cut. She was married and had five kids, and she was a great listener. While growing up, Cindy's home life was a lot like Karrie's, so they quickly became each other's confidants.

"I'll split the tip with you," Cindy said. "That was a big order."

"Thanks." Karrie opened her locker and pulled out her bag.

"Are you excited about seeing Tom tonight?"

"More nervous than excited," Karrie said. "He wants me to meet his college friends. We've been dating for five years, but since he's has been at college, I feel as if this is our first date. I still smell like onions from this morning. Do you have any hand cream?"

"Sure." Cindy handed her a plastic tube of lilac cream. Karrie squeezed a large amount on her hands and rubbed them vigorously.

"Are you going to wear that?" Cindy looked down at Karrie's uniform pants.

"Unfortunately, I am, even though they are stained. I had to go to San Diego State University this morning to talk to a counselor about transferring. I wore my best white pants, which was a mistake because my period came right when standing in line at San Diego State's admission office. Then I fell off a curb. I think I wet myself as well. I ruined my pants, and I was so embarrassed. I don't know if I'm going to have the courage to go back to campus."

"Sure, you will. I bet not as many people noticed as you thought. Besides, everyone's taking their final exams this time of year. People are so involved in their studies that they're not thinking about anyone else." Cindy opened her locker and pulled out a pair of green slacks. "They may be a bit old-fashioned for you, but I think they'll go well with your blue blouse, and they're a lot cuter than your uniform pants."

"Thanks." Karrie looked at the clock again. "I hope I have time to put them on before I have to catch the bus."

"Hey, Cindy!" Estelle shouted from the doorway. "Are you working today or having a tea party with your friend?"

"On my way!" Cindy closed her locker. "I hope Isabella gets back from her maternity leave soon. I don't know if I can stand much more of Estelle as a manager. Who was the manager when Isabella had her first child?"

"I think it was Alejandro. Boy, time passes fast. I've got to get going."

"Why are you taking the bus?"

"This morning, Tom told me his plane was getting in late, so I told him Isabella said she'd drop me off after work. Then I got a text from Isabella that she had gone into labor. I texted Tom, but he hasn't answered. He's usually good about answering his phone, but he didn't today. By default, I'm taking the bus."

"I have to get back out there, but don't worry about the pants. You look great. That French braid flatters your face. He'll be glad to see you, and it'll all be fine."

Karrie ran into the bathroom and changed her pants. She stood sideways and looked at herself in the mirror. The pants didn't look half bad. With her new blue blouse, she looked quite fashionable.

She texted Tom again, saying she might be late because she planned to take the bus. She ran to the curb just as the bus pulled up. It was rush hour, so the bus was packed. Two men in the back were arguing over some political issue, so Karrie stayed near the front. She sat beside a mother with a crying child.

"Sorry, he's fussy today."

"It's okay. I prefer fussy children to fussy adults."

The people around her chuckled. Karrie hadn't realized she'd spoken so loudly but she wasn't embarrassed about it. Instead, she was astonished that people listened to her. It felt powerful.

Soon, the bus stopped a few blocks from the Spaghetti Factory, where she was going to meet Tom. Karrie checked her phone. Tom still hadn't returned her text. It was six o'clock, and Tom wanted her to meet there at 5:30. The restaurant looked crowded. Maybe he was still waiting to be seated.

She hurried down the block to the restaurant and checked her phone again. She had a text from a number she didn't recognize.

<where you @>

<who are you?> She texted back.

No answer. She put her phone back into her purse and took a deep breath as she walked into the restaurant. She scanned the room of people but couldn't see Tom anywhere.

She approached the host, "I'm looking for a friend. It would be under the name Tom Bremen."

"Oh yeah," the host said. "The kid making the puns. They're in the back room."

"Thanks." Karrie pushed through the crowd of laughing people to the back room. In a corner sat a table full of college-aged kids laughing and talking loudly. Josh noticed Karrie first and got up to greet her.

"Karrie, you look so good." He gave her a slight hug and kissed her cheek.

"You look good too. I know it's only been a year, but you've changed into the perfect college student." Karrie scanned the table looking for Tom. He sat on the far side of the table. When their eyes met, he stood up and waved for her to sit next to him.

As she headed toward Tom, he said, "Hey, everyone. This is Karrie, one of our friends from San Diego."

The people nodded and smiled, introducing themselves as Karrie sat down. Her heart sank that he hadn't introduced her as his girlfriend.

"Did you get my text? Tom whispered as she sat down. "No, and I've been texting you all day." She moved her chair closer to Tom, hoping he would put his arm around so everyone at the table would know they were a couple. It bothered her that he hadn't hugged or kissed her when she entered the room. Josh recognized her before Tom did. Something was wrong. "I got a text, but I wasn't sure who it was from." She pulled out her phone and showed it to Tom. "See."

"Oh, that's my number." A tanned blonde girl next to Tom answered. Her tan and hair color matched so perfectly that it was hard to tell where her hair stopped, and her skin began. She had piercing green eyes and was impeccably dressed in a dark plaid blazer with a black velvet collar.

"He lost his phone, so I let him borrow mine. Tom's always losing things."

"Karrie, this is my friend Page. She's in our prayer group at school," Tom said.

"Hey, Page." Karrie moved closer to Tom. "When I didn't hear from you, I grabbed a bus from work. That's why I'm late."

"The bus? In this neighborhood?" Page gasped. "Is that safe?"

"Don't we believe that God will protect us?" Tom finally put his arm around Karrie's shoulder.

"Come on, Tom. You know that's not what I'm talking about," Page said. "Of course, God will protect us, but we have to use our brains."

"Lots of people have to take the bus, Page. It doesn't mean they're brainless." Karrie was surprised at the sternness in her own voice.

"Of course not. That's not what I meant. I didn't mean to be offensive." Page gently tapped her spoon on a glass of water. "Everyone needs to say, "Shame on you" to Tom for not texting Karrie sooner, which forced her into taking the bus."

The group complied, each mocking in turn and wagging their fingers at Tom and saying, "Shame, shame, shame."

Tom stood up and bowed to Karrie. "I humbly apologize, my lady."

Everyone clapped. Karrie blushed and waved Tom away.

"I'm okay. It's fine." She picked up her menu. "Seriously, Karrie. I am so excited to meet you," Page said. "I've heard so much about you. Tom says you're a real woman of God."

"I don't know if that's true. Tom can exaggerate sometimes."

"No, I don't," Tom said. "If I told you about how Karrie trusted God in spite of where she came from—"

Karrie squeezed his arm and shook her head.

"Anyway, she's the best Christian I know."

Once again, he didn't call her his girlfriend.

"Tell me about this prayer group you belong to," Karrie said as she looked over her menu.

"It's exactly what it's called." Tom leaned back, moving away from Karrie. "We meet every Wednesday afternoon, and we made a covenant against using foul language and—"

"Anxious attitudes." Page completed Tom's sentence. She started counting on her fingers. "Keeping the faith, memorizing scriptures, and—of course—no bitterness, strife, or anger."

"Of course." Karrie forced a smile. "That sounds like a good group."

"Tom and I had a causal group like that in high school with Lo'laini and Karrie," Josh said from across the table. "Remember, Karrie?"

"I do." She put down her menu. "That was a great group." Karrie looked at Page, who smiled awkwardly at Tom. "That's a beautiful bracelet, Page. Where did you get it?"

"A year ago, in Maui. My folks took us there to celebrate my high school graduation. Have you ever vacationed there?"

"No, my family doesn't take vacations, generally. But my best friend, Lo'laini, is from Hawaii, and her grandmother said that one day she'd help me to buy a plane ticket to visit Lo'laini when she's back from school. Right now, Lo'laini is in the UK with her aunts. She'll be going to Oxford next year."

"That's impressive." Page leaned her chin on her hands. "Where do you go to school?"

"I just finished a year at a community college. I plan to go to San Diego State University next year. I checked out the campus today and got some business done with the financial aid office."

"My parents went to San Diego State," Page said.

There was an awkward moment of silence between Karrie and Page. The friends chattered around the table, talking about professors and late-night library stories.

"That's another thing you and Page have in common," Tom said, breaking the silence. "You're both prayer warriors. Page had a great answer to prayer that I know you'd like to hear about."

"No, Tom," Page said. "I don't think now is the time to talk about it."

"Karrie loves these kinds of stories. Don't you, Kar?" Tom elbowed her.

"Sure." Karrie pushed away her menu. "It doesn't look like our waitress is coming anytime soon, anyway. I like to hear how God moves in people's lives."

"Well, my car broke down. I guess I needed a new alternator. I had run through my monthly allowance, so I prayed for five hundred dollars because that's how much it would cost to install a new alternator," Page beamed. "Then my grandpa called out of the blue and asked if I needed anything. I mean, it was the very day that I prayed, and he offered to buy me a new car!"

"So, your grandpa bought you a new car because he knew that the old one was about to break down," Karrie said dryly.

"But you see how God answered her prayer, don't you?" Tom asked.

"I see that your grandpa called at the right time, and with prayer, timing is everything." Karrie pushed back her chair. "I ran here straight from work, and I didn't have the time to visit the ladies' room. Since the waitress doesn't seem to be coming anytime soon, I think I'll take that opportunity now. Please excuse me."

Karrie got up from the table and picked up her purse and jacket, maintaining a polite smile until the bathroom door closed behind her. Warm tears ran uncontrollably down her cheeks.

When she looked in the mirror, her blouse seemed faded and frumpy. She was mortified to see a white stain on her sleeve. The fussy child on the bus must have thrown up on her and she didn't even know it. She wetted a paper towel and cleaned the stain, but she didn't wring the towel out well and water dripped across the front of her blouse. She zipped up her jacket, trying to figure out how she would explain why she had to wear it through the rest of dinner. "It's not going to work," she whispered to herself.

"I'm sorry, Karrie."

She looked up and saw Page standing behind her.

Page's reflection startled her. She was beautiful, with her perfect hair falling around her shoulders while tiny red and blonde hairs sprung out from Karrie's unraveling French braid. Their reflections in the mirror were so different. The comparison was too much for Karrie to bear. "What are you sorry about?"

"I saw you take your purse and jacket when you left and thought I should come to talk to you. It must be overwhelming to meet all of Tom's friends at once. I told him that you two should have dinner alone and then meet up with us later."

"It's not overwhelming."

"I think that I can fix this. I can tell our friends to go someplace else so you and Tom can be alone. Or better yet, this will be less obvious. I'll tell Tom that he's being insensitive then he can take you somewhere different. We can meet on another night."

"No." Karrie turned around and faced Page. "You don't need to talk to Tom for me. If I have something to say to him, I can say it myself. But you can tell everyone else that I'm not feeling well and have to go home. I got my period today and I worked a long shift. No need to talk to Tom, I'll text Tom from the bus stop."

"You're still going to take the bus?"

"Yes, Page, I am." Karrie rolled her eyes. "People take the bus all the time. They are perfectly safe. There's a whole world outside of your sheltered life."

"I think you're getting the wrong idea." Page grabbed Karrie's arm as she started to leave. "Tom and I aren't together. Not at all."

"Not yet at least." Karrie bolted out the door. She walked with her head down into the midst of an early December rain.

Splat, splat, splat. Her feet slapped on the wet concrete as she headed for the bus stop.

"Please, God, don't let him follow me. Please. I don't want to see him," Karrie whispered a prayer while warm tears and cool rain mixed down her cheeks and chin. As she got to the corner, the bus pulled away. "Great! Now I have to wait for the next one," Karrie sighed in exasperation.

"Kar! Come on, Kar!" Tom's voice echoed down the street. "What are you doing?"

"I'm not going to get away from him," Karrie whispered as she ducked beneath a store awning. She leaned against a shop glass window in hopes of hiding from Tom, but a store clerk tapped on the window and shooed her away like an unwanted fly. When Karrie stepped forward, Tom stood in front of her. The rain flattened his wavy brown hair, the big water drops rolling down his face and into his eyes.

"What are you doing?" Tom asked breathlessly. "Why are you leaving'?"

"Don't know." She looked away so her eyes wouldn't meet his. "Maybe leaving was better than staying."

Tom furrowed his brow.

Karrie looked directly into his eyes. "If I had stayed, I would have said something cruel. I hate it when people are cruel. I've been hurt by cruelty myself, and I don't want to inflict it on anyone else."

"Why would you be cruel? No one was hurting you. What are you talking about?" He shook his head and rain droplets dispersed from his crown like a broken sprinkler. "Page is a little sheltered, but she's not unkind. She just doesn't know how other people live."

"I guess that's the point." Karrie stepped out from the awning to look for the bus. "She doesn't know, and I do."

Tom pulled out his keys. "If you want to leave, I'll drive your home."

"I don't want you to drive me home. I'm fine with the bus. It gives me time to think about things besides jeopardizing my safety," she said in a sing-song voice as she batted her eyelashes. "I mean, God expects us to have brains, you know." She pulled her pass out of her pocketbook when she saw the bus pull in the stop. "Go back in there. They're expecting you. You know it's what you want to do anyway."

Tom put his hands in his pocket and watched Karrie climb the bus stairs. Then he pulled out his phone and began to text as he climbed the stairs after her.

Karrie sat down in the first seat behind the bus driver and looked up to see Tom standing near the bus door, texting his friends.

"What a sensitive guy. Making sure they don't worry about us, eh?" she smirked.

"Kids, I don't care what kind of fight you're having, but there's a fare for this ride." The bus driver glared at Tom.

He pulled an ATM card out of his back pocket, but the bus driver shook his head.

"It's okay," Karrie said. "I've got it. It was a big tip day at work." She opened her pocketbook ng dropped the fare in the box. "Uptown college kid," she said to the bus driver. "He doesn't carry cash." Karrie sat back down on the seat behind the driver.

Tom sat next to her. "Stop it. You're acting like a jealous hag."

"Hag?" Karrie looked at her reflection in the window. "Taken from the word haggard."

Tom wrinkled his forehead.

"That's a good word for me because that's what I am. I'm haggard." Karrie fought back tears.

"What are you saying?" Tom tried to put his arm around her, but she pushed it away.

"I'm practicing etymology, the study of the origin and meaning of words in their proper context. I've been to college too. Even though it's just a community college and not a fancy "sanctified" school like yours, where rich kids prepare themselves for Christian service."

"It's not just rich kids who go there." Tom sighed and put his palms against his eyes. "I didn't mean to call you haggard."

"But that's what I am. I'm haggard and tired. I'm exhausted." Karrie turned and looked directly at him. "I work five hours at Isabell's restaurant and had three hours of school before I show up at work. Most of my study time is on the bus." She pulled a philosophy book out of her purse.

"Lots of people work their way through school in restaurants," Tom said.

"Some people work there all their lives," Karrie whispered.

"But that won't be you."

"What if it were?" She looked back out the window. "Would that make me less fortunate?"

Tom shrugged. "Of course not. I don't get why you're so upset."

"I am upset because I showed up tonight smelling like pepper and onions because I spent four hours in the restaurant fridge cutting onions and peppers. Your friend, Page, smelled like roses."

"What does it matter what either one of you smells like? No one thought any less of you because of where you work."

"Yeah, they did." Karrie put her finger under Tom's jaw and turned his face toward hers. "You know they did. I'm different from everyone sitting at that table, and they pitied me. Because I was in foster care, I was my sole support and never went on a family vacation. I'm not jealous of Page. I'm envious."

"Wha—"

"You said I'm jealous. You got the sin wrong, I'm not jealous of Page. I'm envious."

Tom looked at his feet. Karrie continued looking out the window and whispered, "I am angry, I guess. You don't know this, but Christian girls aren't allowed to be angry. Feminine anger excludes you from all polite Christian company. It's okay if men get angry—people call those convictions—but women don't get the privilege. Remember that fairy tale story about the two princesses? Every time one of them spoke, a pearl fell out of her mouth. Every time the other one spoke, a frog jumped out of her mouth—a gross wet frog. I'm the second kind of princess because I'm angry and no matter how hard I try, no matter how many prayers I pray, I don't get the pearl. My anger comes out like a slimy toad jumping out of my mouth."

"What are you angry about?"

"I'm angry that when Page prayed for her car to be fixed, her grandfather bought her a new one. When I prayed for things to get better with my mom, they got worse. I'm angry because today while I tried juggling school and work, I couldn't find time to go to the bathroom, so while I was standing in line for financial aid, I wet myself. There, in the middle of fashionable San Diego State University, I stepped off a curb and fell. I had to run across campus with urine and menstrual fluid running down the leg of my new pretty white pants. People helped me up. No one laughed at me. I could see their embarrassment for me, and I was beyond embarrassed."

"Karrie." Tom tried to put his arm around her, but Karrie pushed it away.

"I missed the bus this morning, so I had to wait a half hour for the next bus. I didn't want to walk back to my apartment to use the bathroom, so I thought I would hold it. When I got to San Diego State, there was a long line at the financial office. I need a short-term loan to pay tuition for the fall because our rent went up and I have to chip in at home. I don't have a monthly allowance to help cover my school expenses. If Mom and I don't pay rent, we could be homeless. I've lived that way before, and it terrifies me. I've lived with that fear all my life. I didn't want to lose my place in line, so I thought I would hold it. When I got to the front of the line, I tripped over a curb. People helped me up and asked if I was all right. My pants had red and yellow on them like a watercolor painting."

Tom blushed.

"So, you see, I'm not jealous of Page. I'm not jealous of the car her grandfather bought her. I'm envious because no one in my family can buy me a car and we don't go on vacations," Karrie sighed. Raindrops spattered across the glass. "And I'm heartbroken because Page is what every Christian girl is supposed to be. She's the personification of Proverbs thirty-one, and that's what I wanted to be."

"You are a virtuous woman."

"Let me finish," Karrie said. "All my life, I've been waiting for something good to happen to offset everything bad that's happened to me. In church and at Sunday school, teachers and pastors told me it was all about faith and that money and status don't matter. They even told me the abuse didn't make me any less than anyone else because I trusted Jesus and he would make everything okay."

"I believe that too," Tom said. "It doesn't matter what's happened to you. You've already told me how much Christ has healed you."

"But it matters. It matters that I wasn't protected, and Page was. It matters to me that protection and love aren't evenly distributed. As much as I try, I'll never be like Page. Until now, I thought that one day I would be like her, that somehow my faith would make everything even. But faith doesn't make everything even. Some of us have more challenging roads to walk. I used to consume Christian biographies and imagine myself in the lives of those characters. I believed, I really believed, that it would happen to me like it happened to all those Christian women. I could put up with the poverty, going hungry, the stinky house full of animal feces if only one day I knew I grow into that stereotypical Christian woman. The woman with a loving husband and kids and a beautiful home. The church lady who walks around with a placid smile on her face and never challenges the men around her or argues with them."

"You think that's what I want in my wife?"

"I don't know if that's what you want, but it's what I wanted to be, but meeting Page tonight, I realized I'm never going be that girl. That hurt. Something shattered inside of me. I lost a vision of my future. I lost a dream."

"I think you're as good as Page, Karrie."

"I do too. I think I'm better than she is. However, I may not be as good for you as she is. I don't think I am what you really want."

There was another long moment of silence.

"Does Page come from a good Christian family?" Karrie asked.

"I don't know what you're talking about."

"Sure, you do. Every parent wants their kid to marry into a good family. Does Page come from a good family?"

"Her father's an engineer and her mother's a schoolteacher. They go to a megachurch in Pasadena."

"Of course they do." Karrie looked Tom directly in his eyes. "I don't come from a good family. We struggle with alcoholism and abuse. I think I am as good as Page is, maybe better, for keeping my faith in the midst of my abuse, but I'm different from her. That's what hurts right now. It hurts me that I'm different. My experience made me different, and it was an experience I didn't choose. I don't fit into the same crowd as you do, and I really wanted to fit in tonight. You don't know how badly I wanted to fit in."

"Karrie, you're having this fight with yourself and not with me." Tom's voice cracked and tears fell down his cheek.

"Maybe, but I think you want to be with Page right now."

"At least there's less drama when I'm with her." Tom looked out the window again.

"Exactly! Because she's been protected, and I wasn't given that gift."

"Karrie," Tom groaned while rubbing his eyes.

"Did you really make a vow to your prayer group with Page not to use any swear words?" Karrie smiled at him.

"Yep."

She changed the tone of her voice. "So anyway, these fish were swimming really fast in a lake and they hit a big concrete wall, and you know what they said?"

Tom smirked and lifted one eyebrow. "Dam?"

"I made you break your vow." The bus pulled up to the curb near Karrie's apartment. "This is my stop." She got up and ran out the door shouting over her shoulder, "You can take an Uber to get home."

"Whatever." Tom stumbled off the bus. Karrie could feel him watching her until she got to her door. She turned around after she got to the door. Through her tear-blurred eyes, Tom looked like a smudged watercolor painting melting in the rain.

†

Chapter Fourteen

A Significant Conversation

Karrie

"I'm sorry, but Pastor Mike isn't here for the next three weeks." Mrs. Write looked up from her appointment book. "How are you doing, Karrie?"

"I'm fine. Do you know when he'll be back?"

"Not for a few months. He's on a sabbatical."

The words hit Karrie like a brick as she stood trembling in the church's office doorway, trying to fight back tears.

"I walked five miles all the way from home to talk to him."

"Why don't you sit down, and I'll get you a water bottle? You look exhausted."

"No, I'll just go home." Karrie started to leave when Mrs. Write stood in her way, looking at her with concern, she said,

"Wait a minute. Maybe Pastor Lydia could talk to you." She waved at someone in the hallway behind Karrie.

"Is someone talking about me?" Pastor Lydia asked.

Lydia was a tall, wiry middle-aged woman with long gray-blonde hair loosely tied in a bun on the back of her head. Karrie had seen Lydia in the foyer of the church on previous Sundays. Karrie recognized her by her distinctive laugh. Everyone noticed Pastor Lydia when she came into a room.

"I heard my name. Hey, Karrie. How are you?"

"I'm okay."

"You don't look okay. Why don't you come into my office, and we can talk a bit?"

Pastor Lydia opened her office door and beckoned Karrie inside. Karrie reluctantly walked inside her office and stood in the middle while Pastor Lydia motioned for her to sit in a chair. Karrie stood, making two small fists to stop her fingers from shaking. She bit her lower lip, hoping it would stop her sniffles from a night of crying.

"I've heard you had a rough couple of days."

Karrie felt betrayed. "How did you know?"

"Mrs. Bremen attends my women's Bible study."

"Of course, Tom told her about it." Karrie looked resentfully at the ground. "I'm here to talk to Pastor Mike. I don't believe women should be pastors."

"That isn't the first time I've heard that sentiment," Pastor Lydia motioned again to a chair. "Sit down. I heard you tell Deanna that you walked all the way here."

"I need to save on bus fare."

"And with that heavy backpack?"

"I've got orientation at three at SDSU, so I stopped here on my way to talk to Pastor Mike. Mrs. Write said he was out, and I should meet with you, but, like I said, I don't believe in women pastors."

"You look like you're about ready to drop. Five miles up El Cajon Boulevard in the hot sun isn't easy. Take a load off."

Karrie moved tentatively toward the chair. Her muscles ached and sweat rolled down her cheeks. Pastor Lydia placed a bottle of water next to the chair. It tempted Karrie to let herself sit, but it felt like that would surrender her principles, so she stood. "I came to see Pastor Mike."

"He's taken a sabbatical."

"How long will he be gone?" Karrie moved closer to the chair.

"A full year."

"That's a long time."

"It can be, especially if you spend the whole time standing." Pastor Lydia put her hands firmly on Karrie's shoulders, gently pushing down and laughed. "Please, sit down."

Pastor's Lydia's calming laugh made Karrie smile. She leaned back into the plush chair. Her throbbing body relaxed. Karrie grabbed the water and took a big swig. "Sorry," she said between gulps. "But I'm really thirsty."

"I figured you might be. As I said, I've heard you had a couple of rough days."

"I've had a couple of rough years, but I don't want to talk about that yet." She wiped her face with both hands, clearing away the warm sweat and some straggling strands of hair that dangled in her eyes. She took a deep breath, and then said, "I want to know how you justify it?"

"Justify what? What are you talking about?" Lydia asked.

"Well, you're a woman?"

"Yes, a fact that my husband is most happy about." Pastor Lydia chuckled as she sat down on the chair across from Karrie.

"That wasn't what I was talking about." Karrie took a deep breath. "You're also a preacher. The bible says women can't be preachers."

Pastor Lydia smiled as she examined Karrie from head to toe. "Now, that is a longer conversation than I think that we have time for today. There are more pressing matters that brought you into this office to talk."

"What could be more pressing than the Bible? Scripture's clear about why God created women!" Karrie's harsh voice startled even her. It sounded like someone else's voice. There was something of her mother's anger in her voice, and Karrie didn't like it. That anger made her stomach churn.

But Karrie didn't only hear her mother in her angry retort to Pastor Lydia. She heard the anger of every Christian woman who had lectured her on submission. "The Supportive Role of Women" had been preached to Karrie throughout her life, but something about Pastor Lydia's existence questioned the validity of those sermons. Pastor Lydia's independence was new and different from the other church women Karrie knew.

For a while, she'd questioned her mother's view of submission and how it affected Karrie. Before she fought with Tom, she argued with her mother about changing her major, which led to another fight over her father returning home and her mother's insistence that Karrie was bitter because she didn't want him to live with them. Her mother had weaponized the words "bitterness" and "unsupportive" into piercing knives that cut into Karrie's soul. Her mother's screaming voice still echoed in her head. "Forgive and forget!"

Five years earlier, anger had filled her mother's voice in defense of Karrie's father in the judge's chambers when Karrie had been placed into foster care. Her brother and father were entitled to anger, which Karrie was expected to forgive. She learned early on that men's lives, desires, and ambitions were more important than hers. Their pride had to be respected and their futures protected. She wasn't allowed the gift of self-respect or self-determination. Karrie had genuinely believed in that pecking order, where men were over women. It was a Christian value she defended. Pastor Lydia's role at the church threatened that order.

"You are quite certain that you know why God created women?" Pastor Lydia asked Karrie. "You think there's only one purpose for women's creation?"

Karrie lifted her gaze from the ground and looked at Pastor Lydia.

"I can see that this is a conversation you've been having with yourself for quite a long time now." Pastor Lydia leaned in. "Women weren't simply created for the support and pleasure of men, as a lot of Christians have been errantly taught. God created men and women in the image of God to be loved and cared for by Him. He gave both of them stewardship over this earth. Both were given the ten commandments and were taught to protect their children by behaving righteously toward them. Both were given salvation and forgiveness through Jesus Christ and the great commission, but most importantly, both are equally loved by God. That teaching is found in Genesis One, twenty-six through thirty and Galatians three, twenty-two through twenty-nine. I can provide you with more scriptures if you want, but I think you have something more important pressing on your heart today."

"How come some people get protected while some of us cry out into the night and there is no answer?" Karrie's eyes welled up in tears.

"I don't know, Karrie. Some people have easier lives than others. I am sorry. What happened to you as a child was not fair."

Karrie wept.

"I heard you give your testimony five years ago."

"Everyone told me how brave I was." Karrie drew a tissue from the box near her chair and blew her nose. "That felt really good."

"The nose blowing or the affirmation of your bravery?" Pastor Lydia smiled.

"Both," Karrie laughed. "The nose blowing, the water, the soft chair, and the encouragement people gave me."

"I'm glad you received that affirmation. You were brave, but no child should have to be that brave. Others should have protected you. You should have received the love you needed while growing up."

Karrie nodded. "I think my mom loves me. It's just..." Karrie looked out the window as the wind battered a palm tree. "Maybe she loves other stuff more."

"Something inside of her is broken, and it prohibits her from taking care of you." Pastor Lydia tried to catch Karrie's eye.

"Yeah," Karrie whispered. She looked at the tree outside as Pastor Lydia looked at her.

"Like I said when you first came in," Pastor Lydia said. "I heard you had a rough week. Do you want to talk about it?"

"I guess I feel like my life has always been rough, and I'm sick of it. I'm frightened that it's not going to get any better."

Karrie poured out her story. She described the abuse and the foster care system and the reunification with her mother. Between sobs, she told Pastor Lydia about the awkward date with Tom, his perfect friend Page, her infuriating conversation with Page in the bathroom and how abandoned she felt at the restaurant. Lastly, she shared about the breakup with Tom on the bus.

"It's always the same with me. I'm always on the outside looking in. It's so unfair." Karrie looked at Pastor Lydia directly, "How come some people get more love than others?"

"That was a lot." Pastor Lydia took off her glasses and wiped a tear away. They both looked at the windblown tree. Then Pastor Lydia said, "The short answer is that you're right, life isn't fair. Life isn't fair because sin entered this world, and people often suffer because of other people's sins. You've had more than your fair share of suffering. Your parents' sins are more than the way they treat you. It's the way they perceive you as well. Sin affects not only our actions but our perceptions. Our perceptions of other people influence how we treat them."

Pastor Lydia looked Karrie straight in the eye. "Your mother and father have an incorrect perception of you, a cruel and wrong perception of you. They don't see you as someone who should be protected, so they don't protect you. They see you as someone who should meet their needs. You know that's not the way it's supposed to work. Adults are supposed to meet their children's needs. Children cannot meet adults' needs."

"Sometimes Mom tried to protect me." Karrie looked down at her hands.

"Sometimes," Pastor Lydia said. "But from what you've told me, it wasn't enough. They didn't protect you enough so you could feel safe."

"So, what should be my response? I love my mom, so I don't want to be angry at her. She needs me, you know." Karrie looked at again at the pastor.

"You can be angry at people who you love, Karrie." Pastor Lydia smiled. "I don't think your mom needs you as much as you think she does. Anger is a gift from God, and it's a useful emotion. It helps us protect ourselves and the people we love. Righteous anger can help us advocate against injustice and for the vulnerable in this world."

"It sounds weird putting those two words together, righteous and anger."

"Those two words belong together in the Bible. Righteous anger was what the prophets felt when they spoke against the abuse of women and children and foreigners in Jeremiah, Obadiah, and Isaiah. Protection and anger have a lot in common. Let me explain it this way. If you were a person who was protected by loving parents when you were a child, your parents would get angry if someone got in your space or threatened you. By witnessing their protective behavior, you'd learn self-protection. Protective parents teach their children safety. But if a child gets used to their parents mistreating them, they might perceive mistreatment as normal. They may even mistake sarcasm for love. Any anger an abused child feels is stifled because anger can bring on more abuse. Karrie, you weren't protected as a child and should have been. I think you're feeling some of the outrage from your childhood neglect. The anger you feel toward your mom is righteous anger, and I don't think you should squash it. But you should learn to control it and nurture it so you can use it to protect yourself. As a Christian minister, it bothers me that in some Christian circles, righteous anger is hushed by false whispers of forgiveness. This is often used to silence the abuse of women. Hushing people's pain and not attending to the injustice that caused their pain is cruel. The prophet Jeremiah calls it *healing the people lightly."*

"It's funny. All I've ever heard in the church was that scriptures commanded me not to be angry," Karrie smiled.

"Do you know there is a scripture that tells you to be angry? It's found in Ephesians. It talks about expressing your anger at the appropriate time. Great sins have been committed against you, Karrie, and I think right now you are learning to protect yourself and develop judgment, so you don't fall into the same patterns as your parents."

"What happens when you can't be angry at the appropriate time?"

"Is that what happened to you? Do you want to tell me about it?" Pastor Lydia leaned in.

"There's not much to tell. I knew if I got angry at my mother, brothers, and father, the hitting would start. Once it started, I never knew how it would end. I had to hush my anger and act like their cruel words and actions didn't hurt me."

"Now you carry that "hushed anger" around inside you?"

"Yeah, I can't seem to unleash it on anyone else, so I give it to myself most of the time."

"I think the greatest tragedy of abuse is the self-blame that lingers. Your healing journey will include learning to hand responsibility for your abuse back to your parents so you can pass it on to the generation after you. That's why I feel it's toxic for Christians to talk about forgiveness too early in the healing process.

Before we go on, let's define forgiveness. Forgiveness takes place when a person chooses not to take revenge for an unjust action inflicted upon them by the act of their will. To forgive, you must first admit that you have been harmed. With that acknowledgment comes the understanding that the person who harmed you is dangerous. That acknowledgment can help promote the voice of caution and sober judgment, two characteristics the book of Proverbs encourages believers to practice. Forgiveness doesn't mean you have to trust someone who's proven themself untrustworthy."

"So, I shouldn't feel guilty about wanting to move out of my mother's house?"

"No, you must certainly should not."

"But my anger flares up a lot, especially now that I'm getting older."

"Especially in romantic relationships?"

Karrie blushed and nodded.

"My guess is you're learning to practice discernment in your romantic relationships, and that brings up memories of how your parents didn't protect or love you as a child. When that anger flares up in your romantic relationships, don't completely hush it. You can learn from it. It can teach you to demand respect from your romantic partners. That's ultimately what God wants for you, and I think it's what you really want for yourself. Don't hush that voice. Use it to keep unsafe people away from you. Anger can teach you who you should trust and who you should not trust. As far as your abuse is concerned, the forgiveness of your father and mother might be a lifelong journey. In Matthew eighteen, twenty-one through twenty-two, Peter asked Jesus how many times he must forgive someone. Jesus said seven times seventy. That equation was the symbolic number for eternity in the Hebrew language. I think this scripture teaches us that forgiveness is a process. There are some violations that are so egregious and damaging that we might have to spend the rest of our lives giving them to God and asking Him to teach us how to forgive them. By forgiving someone's offense, I don't mean trusting the offender again, mind you. I mean surrendering the people who abused you to God and trusting Him to correct the offender, relieving yourself of the task of trying to correct and protect people who cannot be fixed because they refuse to repent. Because forgiveness is a continual action, Jesus used the equation seven times seventy that means eternity. You're not expected to trust someone who has proven themselves untrustworthy again and again and again."

Karrie nodded.

Pastor Lydia looked compassionately at Karrie. "I wish every person got the love they deserve here on earth."

Karrie stretched her arms above her head and sighed, then smiled at Pastor Lydia. She looked at her phone. "Oh my gosh. My class begins in thirty minutes. I have to get going."

"One more thing. We've talked about the great sins that have been committed against you, but you also told me about some ordinary things that happened to you over the past few days that I want to address with you. You broke up with a guy whom you loved. That happens to most people in their lives. You fell in love with a boy, and for a time, he loved you back. It was a gift to you in the middle of the darkness of foster care dealing with your mother's irresponsibility and the aftereffects of your father's abuse."

"You're talking in the past tense as if Tom and I are over! I guess I'm still hoping we can get back together."

"There are a few questions I would like you to ask yourself about your date the other night before you consider getting back together, Tom."

Karrie nodded.

"First of all, let me say that Page's life may not be as perfect as you imagine. You don't know what's going on inside her or what struggles she has faced."

"She hasn't gone through what I went through."

"Would you want her to?" Pastor Lydia leaned forward. "Would you really wish that upon her? No one should have to go through what you did. From what you've told me, it sounds like she was as frightened of you as you were of her. Two women competing over one man is a bad idea. There are bound to be conflicts. Both of you managed it as well as you could."

Karrie shrugged.

"I see that I'm not getting through to you on this point. But I also think you were wrong when you told Tom you wouldn't be good for him because of your family. I don't think you're as damaged as you perceive yourself to be. When it comes to marriage, it isn't necessary to come from a good family to marry a decent Christian guy. It's only necessary that you have within you the desire to learn how to create a good family. As Christians, we believe in transformation and redemption, so our birth family doesn't have to dictate the kind of family we create as adults. Women with your past abuse get married all the time and sometimes to pretty nice guys. You're treating yourself as damaged goods, but that isn't how God sees you. It's not how most people see you. Don't let classism define you. It's not scriptural. It's wrong and does a lot of damage. Don't do that Karrie, don't do that to anyone."

Pastor Lydia's voice shook. She looked at the same tree that had captivated Karrie for the last half hour. "Beware the sin of writing people off because of their backgrounds, Karrie. Church history is full of ugly examples of what happens when Christians give in to that kind of bigotry and cruelty. If you exclude yourself from certain blessings because of your background, you will eventually exclude others. Don't do that. Don't rob people of something the grace of God freely gives them: the equity of being created in God's image. Heaven knows the world does that enough. It's cruel to judge people by their cars, their education, their looks, friends, or family. Don't go there. That kind of classism and bigotry leaves wounds that haunt people for the rest of their lives," her voice cracked. "Our values may work that way, but God's economy does not."

Karrie was surprised at Pastor Lydia's voice crack. For a moment, she felt she got a glimpse of the woman beneath Pastor Lydia's strong professional veneer.

Karrie remembered in the group home when Lo'laini first told her about Pastor Lydia before Karrie started to go to church with Lo'laini. Lo'laini had woken Karrie up after she got home from a retreat because she had some hot gossip about the new pastor at church. She had heard it from the adults when they didn't think children were listening. Ms. Write and Pastor Lydia drove Lo'laini back to the group home after the youth retreat. Lo'laini had dozed off but woke up to Ms. Write and Pastor Lydia whispering about her first call in Christian ministry.

"She's like us," Lo'laini excitedly whispered. "She came from a home like ours!" Lo'laini started unpacking her things while talking about the juicy story she'd heard. "I mean, she looks so good when she stands up in church like nothing has ever hurt her. But that's not true, from what I heard tonight."

"What did you hear?"

"Pastor Lydia was saying she had it rough growing up. She lived in a neighborhood where she got beat up at school and it was tough at home. When she got out of high school, she felt a call to go into Christian service. I know that's not surprising,"

Lo'laini got an emery board and started to file her nails as she continued to speak in a hushed tone. "In high school, Pastor Lydia got this internship at the community theater where everyone treated her really good. After graduation, she took another internship at a Christian community theater. She said it was a nightmare. There was this guy she worked with in the mail room who totally harassed her. He mocked and ridiculed her for the way she dressed and where she grew up. He would steal her things and hide them, then yell at her for every little mistake she made. Nothing like that happened when she worked in the secular theater. She was totally accepted there, and no one cared about her family's background. She said if anyone had bullied a woman the way she was bullied, someone would've talked to him, but it wasn't true in the Christian theater. Mocking the differences between men and women was acceptable, and so was snubbing people if they didn't go to the right school or have the right family connections. She said it bothered her for years that Christians were more class conscience than non-Christians. But it doesn't shock me." Lo'laini laughed. "You can find snotty people everywhere. Anyway, the final blow came at a meeting when there was a discussion about women in ministry. The jerk in the mail room got really angry and kept bugging her about it all day long. In the middle of his rantings, she closed a drawer and a box of papers fell off the top of the filing cabinet." Lo'laini stopped filing her nails and leaned toward Karrie, and whispered, "He hit her."

"He what?" Karrie sat up in bed.

"She said it was more like a slug, but nobody did anything. They stood around and stared at her. They seemed to feel sorry for her, but nobody did anything."

"I know that feeling." Karrie wrapped herself tighter in her blanket.

"This is what really shocked me. Pastor Lydia told Ms. Write, "I was used to my parent's abuse, but I never thought it would happen in a Christian ministry. It was the most disempowering and shaming moment in my life.""

"I guess it can happen anywhere," Karrie whispered. "What did she do?"

"I suppose she did what everyone does when they get hit unexpectedly. She tried not to fall down so she wouldn't get hurt worse."

Karrie laid back in bed. "I hate that feeling when you're so shocked that you can't do anything. I hate it when someone tells me if they got hit, they would hit back."

"People who say that have never been hit before, in public or in an unexpected place. They don't know what it feels like to have the air knocked out of them or have their knees buckle while trying to grab onto something, so they don't humiliate themselves any more by falling. It's not like a schoolyard brawl where someone's been talking smack and you're ready to hit back. It stuns you, and you've got to get control of the situation, so you don't get hurt worse. I hate it when people say what they would do if someone hit them. No one knows how they'd respond when that first blow comes, so people act all tough like it could never happen to them. But the first blow isn't about toughness. It's about survival and getting control of the situation. But anyway, Pastor Lydia said she kept her calm. She fought back tears, trying desperately not to make a bigger scene than what had already played out. She told him never to hit her again. But she also told Ms. Write that she hated the way she told him. She used this soft voice, the kind gentle voice that Christian women are taught to use. She said it made her stomach turn."

"I know that voice," Karrie said.

"So do I… my mom uses it when my dad gets angry. I hate that voice. I hate that Christian women have to use that voice."

"After that, did they fire him?"

"No," Lo'laini said. "Instead, they got rid of her, and they were cruel in the way they did it."

"What do you mean?" Karrie sat up and turned on the lamp next to her.

"In this ministry, members were supposed to raise their own financial support. Pastor Lydia had written a one-woman show where she played different women in the Bible. She staged it and even got some local singers to add music to it. Her church let her perform on a Sunday night. She spent the little bit of money that she had to publicize it and send out letters to raise support. At the end of her performance, she showed a brief video about the theater ministry, and her church took an offering for her support. They not only gave her a really big offering, but the mission committee gave her a year's salary to provide for her needs while she worked at the theater company. But get this. When the theater company got the funds, they wouldn't give it to her. They told her since she showed a video about the Christian theater at the end of her performance, the theater had the right to take all the money the church had given her, leaving her nothing to live on. They even charged her for the flyers she ran off to publicize her show and took all profits for themselves, even though they contributed nothing to the show."

"Wow." Karrie rubbed her eyes. "What did she say when they did that?"

"I guess not a lot. Remember, I was pretending to be asleep while they talked about this, so I didn't see their faces. But Pastor Lydia said she'd been taught to be submissive while growing up, so it was hard for her to protest. She said she tried to confront them, but no one took her seriously. Ms. Write said they were callously cruel, and Pastor Lydia said it devastated her and shook her faith."

Lo'laini described how emotional Pastor Lydia had become when she explained everything.

"I bet they wouldn't have treated her that way if she had come from a wealthier family," Karrie said. "They did it because she came from a place like us. She didn't dress right or go to private bible college. They were trying to get rid of her to cover up what that guy did, and they knew the money was an easy way to do it because she had none. Christians are supposed to act differently, but sometimes they don't."

"Pastor Lydia said they snubbed her in every other way, so she wanted out of there. During her final audition with them, she broke character so she could leave the company without having to explain herself. But then she told Ms. Write that she wished she could say abuse didn't happen in the church, but it happens more than she'd like to say."

"You know they didn't want you to hear that, girl," Karrie laughed.

"That's why I pretended I was asleep. But what pastor Lydia said next is what got to me. She sighed and said, "Misogyny, classism, dishonesty. Those things are everywhere. You can't hide from them even when you're in Christian service."" Lo'laini turned off the light, climbed into bed, and whispered, "Pastor Lydia said the one thing she learned from that place was that no one could take her call away from her, and she was going to make sure it never happened again. Even though it did happen, and because of that, sometimes her jaw still quivers when someone gets angry at her, especially at church."

"From the hit?" Karrie asked.

"From the slug," Lo'laini said.

"Are you still with me, Karrie?" Pastor Lydia's voice brought Karrie back to the present.

Karrie looked at Pastor Lydia's jaw as she stood. Her voice was firm and calm. Karrie blushed at her own criticism of Pastor Lydia as wiry and thin. Karrie had not thought of Pastor Lydia's feelings when she blurted out her criticism of her. Her old church taught her that women could not teach or preach, and yet she was being taught by a woman in a way that no man had ever taught her. She now saw Pastor Lydia as a person. A person who had more than one door slammed in her face.

She'd been shamed for her background when she first entered the ministry and had probably felt the familiar jabs that were hurled at other women in ministry. Still, she stood firmly, fulfilling her vocation.

"Are you listening to me?" Lydia asked again.

"Yeah," Karrie said. "My mind wandered for a moment."

"Come back completely because what I want to tell you is important. I don't think the fight you had with Tom last night was about where you grew up or your class differences."

"What do you mean?"

"I have a question for you, Karrie. If Page had not arrived at the restaurant that night and it was just you and Tom, do you think that you two would have still fought? Would you still have broken up with him?"

Pastor Lydia's question stunned Karrie.

"He's changed a lot since he went away to school, hasn't he? And so have you. I've watched you in church since you started college. You're much more empowered than you were in high school. Tom was a beautiful gift to you for three years. He provided you with a lot of laughter and fun."

"And affection," Karrie said.

"Of course, affection," said Pastor Lydia. "That's the gift of young love."

"I thought I would marry him," Karrie whispered.

"Not a bad hope or daydream for a girl struggling with foster care and reuniting with her parents. But maybe that gift was for a short time. Maybe the relationship has run its course, and it might be time to let this friendship go. I wouldn't call Tom "paper thin," as Lo'laini said, but I don't think he's as deep as you'd like him to be. Maybe Tom hasn't moved as far away from you as you have from him. You've talked too much about whether you are good for Tom, it's time to start thinking about whether Tom is good for you."

Karrie looked at the palm tree outside. The wind stopped, and the tree stood straight in perfect stillness.

†

Chapter Fifteen

Isabella's good-bye

Agostina: Homecoming

"Thanks for calling me," Isabella said as she opened the door to the nursing home. "I'm glad I could rush over right away. Is it true? Mom is talking again?"

"Yes," Michelle said, getting up from the receptionist's desk to hug Isabella. "She's talking as if she woke up from a dream."

"Is she out of her bed and walking?"

"No, she's still too weak to walk, but it's as if she's a different person. I'll take you there." Michelle led Isabella down the hall. "You're lucky you got here today. I don't think we'll be admitting visitors tomorrow. We had a meeting today about that bat virus. I think they'll put us on lockdown for the next few weeks, which means no visitors."

"Oh, the coronavirus," Isabella laughed. "I wouldn't worry about it. It's just another virus like the flu. I think people are making mountains out of molehills. It'll be over in a few days like yesterday's news."

"I hope you're right," Michelle said as they turned the corner.

Outside Agostina's room, Dr. Harness leaned against the wall, writing on a chart. "Isabella, I'm so glad I caught you." She closed the chart. "I want to talk to you about your mother's condition."

"Can it wait?" Isabella passes by the doctor into her mother's room. "I want to see Mom; I want to hear her voice again. She stopped talking weeks before she came here, and it's been so long." She entered the room to an empty bed and her breath stopped.

"Don't worry," Dr. Harness said. "That's her roommate's bed. Agostina is behind the screen. But I do want to warn you not to be too optimistic. Oftentimes cancer patients rally before they—"

Ignoring the doctor's words, Isabella pushed away the screen and saw her mother bathed in sunlight, smiling, and sitting up in bed humming a hymn. Her face glowed from the afternoon sunlight that poured through the window and reflected off her sheets.

"Oh, Mija" Agostina gasped, opening her arms.

Isabella tearfully melted into her mother's embrace. "Mama. Mama," she cried. "You've been gone so long."

"Have I?" Agostina asked, wiping away a tear. "Yes, I have. Too long. It felt as if I were stuck in a wall. I could see and hear things around me but didn't understand them. I've wished so many times these years that someone would pull me out of the wall. Isabella, I've remembered too. So many memories I thought I had lost to the blurriness of time. Things I should have told you many years ago."

"It doesn't matter, Mama. It doesn't matter now because I'm going to take you home. It was a mistake to bring you here."

Isabella turned and looked directly at the doctor. "My mama is not going through a rallying phase. I know healing when I see one."

Dr. Harness smiled, "I hope so." She looked down at her phone. "Someone is buzzing me. We can talk later if you'd like."

"If we do," Isabella said. "It will be about taking my mama home."

"I have so much to tell you, Mija. Remember when you were a first-year student in college and were angry at me because I didn't tell you we were Guatemalan, not Mexican? And I had never told you about your father."

"Mama, it doesn't matter now. I was young and stupid. You were always a good mother, and you always worked hard to let me know you loved me. I have two servers whose parents have not taken care of them the way you cared for me, and it shows in their insecurities. It shows how frightened they are of the world. Mama, I thank God that you were there for me."

"Yes, Maja, but I kept things from you. Remember how it made you angry?"

"I behaved like a brat back then, so please forget it." Isabella leaned in and put her face next to her mom's. "You have two grandchildren now. A grandson was born three years ago, and a granddaughter was born two weeks ago."

"A little boy and a little girl," Agostina sighed. "Does your little girl look like my little girl?"

Isabella tearfully nodded.

"You were a beautiful child. So strong and resilient. You made that journey with me, Mija. Did I ever tell you that?" Agostina took Isabella's hands. "That long horrible journey from the wars in Guatemala. You traveled with me, and you were my joy the whole time. I didn't tell you about the journey because I couldn't tell you." She teared up.

"For years, it was too painful to speak about because all I could remember were the struggle, bloodshed, hardship, and fighting. Don't you see? I didn't want to give you the hardship, so I didn't talk about it. It's not bad for a mother to protect her daughter from the nightmares of this world, is it?"

"No, of course not, Mama. It doesn't matter. That's all in the past."

Isabella looked at her phone, which had been going off since she entered the room.

"But by protecting you from the hard memories, I left out the good memories. I never told you about my pretty pink house that smelled like fresh mint or Abisai. My dear Abisai. He was your father. Did I tell you about him?"

"Yes, Mama, you did when we had that fight when I was in college, remember?" Isabella scrolled through the many messages on her phone.

"But I didn't tell you how kind and wonderful he was. He was a poet, and he loved us. Please look at me, Isabella. I want to see the expression on your face when I tell you about him."

"I will look at you, and we'll have a long talk when I get you out of here, but right now, Alejandro is trying to reach me. It's something about the restaurant. He's out of town, and Estella, one of our managers, called him and said we have to close. Something about this virus." Isabella looked back up at Agostina. "Don't worry. You can tell me about it, and we'll talk. I promise. I just have some business to take care of right now."

"Don't go." Agostina looked desperately up at Isabella as she stood up. "Stay. Please stay awhile."

"Nothing to worry about," Isabella said, kissing her mom on the forehead. "I'm just going into the hallway to answer these calls. I'll be right back by your side in a second." She pressed the speed dial to call Alejandro, waved at her mother, and left the room. "Hey, hon. What's up?"

"Sorry to bother you during your visit, babe, but the girls got a notice from the health department."

"You mean the women in our employ got a notice from the health department."

"Sorry, excuse my implied bias against women, dear."

"Forgiven this time," Isabella laughed.

"It was about this Covid thing. I checked our email, and the health department notified us two weeks ago, but with you giving birth and everything, I guess I didn't see it."

"What about Estella? She should have been on top of the emails." Isabella dropped her phone as two nurses rushed by her, brushing against her. "Oops!" Isabell picked up her phone again. "Sorry, hon. Heavy traffic here in this hallway. I'll check the emails when I get home. It'll be rough if we have to shut down for a couple of weeks, but I think we can manage it. I'll call Estella to see what help she needs to inform the staff."

"Thanks, babe. Hey, how's your mom? Is it true? Is she really back?"

"She is, and I want to take her home. I know it might be hard, but we can work out the logistics."

"We'll figure out something. Enjoy your visit."

"Bye." Isabella kissed the phone and placed it back in her handbag, but as she entered her mom's room, her smile vanished.

Dr. Harness blocked her way, a somber expression on her face. "I'm so sorry, Isabella. It was heart failure. She signed a do not resuscitate form. That was before she lapsed into dementia. She was tired of the chemotherapy. It's been six years, but her body had been through so much. I tried to tell you I've seen many cancer patients revive for a short time before their body gives up. There's not much we could do anyway. She was too far gone."

The doctor's words buzzed like a broken television. Isabella pushed the doctor aside and saw her mother lying on the bed… still. Her glow was gone. The pinkness of life had vanished from Agostina's face, replaced by a cold greyness. Her chest sank beneath the hospital gown as her abdomen bloated into a small bump.

"Mama." Isabella cried.

✝

Chapter Sixteen

Karrie's Journey Home

"Okay, everyone." Estella's keys jingled from her armband as she locked the front door and turned on the neon "Closed" sign. "Gather in the break room before you take off tonight. I have an announcement."

Servers and kitchen staff groaned, then shuffled into the break room after cleaning their stations. It had been a long day, and it had just started to rain. No one wanted to stay after work.

I hope I don't miss my bus. Karrie glanced at the clock on the wall.

"Don't worry about missing your bus," Cindy said as they sat. "Mark lent me the car this evening. I can give you a lift."

Karrie sighed with relief. "Thanks so much. I hate taking the bus this late at night."

"I got a call from Alejandro and Isabella." Estelle's voice rang out over the employee's chit-chat, calling the meeting to order. "It looks like the restaurant is going to be closing its doors on Friday due to the pandemic by order of the health department and city council."

The room grew quiet. Estella swallowed hard as she watched pain and anxiety pass over the faces of the staff.

"One week is short notice, don't you think?" Someone from the kitchen crew shouted.

"Yes, it is. I guess I missed the initial email they sent us two weeks ago, and I only found the notice the health department mailed us last week."

"And who's fault is that?" Someone else yelled.

"Leave her alone," one of the servers said. "She's had a rough week."

"You can blame me if you want to, but I'm in the same boat as all of you. I can't afford this either." Her voice shook as she read from her notes. "Alejandro and Isabella are hoping to open in a few weeks to serve takeout food, but they'll only need a skeleton staff, so there will be some layoffs."

A general groan washed over the staff.

"I'm sorry. They told me to tell you that they're sorry too. Alejandro was out of town when we got the notice, and as you know, Isabella is on maternity leave. She asked me to make sure we have all of your emails so we can have a Zoom meeting to discuss the details. There will be unemployment benefits for those laid off and a small bonus because you served the restaurant. Who knows? "Maybe this won't be for long." Estella swallowed hard again.

"The problem is we don't know how long," Cindy whispered to Karrie. "How am I going to feed my kids?"

They walked slowly to the car amidst whispers of desperation between their workers.

"I dread telling my mom," Karrie said after she got in the car. "I guess this means she's going to lose her paycheck as well."

Cindy turned the ignition key more than once to get her Chevrolet's engine to turn over. "I hope this car's starter isn't going out. That's the last thing we need." Cindy drove out of the parking lot. "I don't think I'll have to tell Mark about this. He predicted it. He said something while we were watching the news last night. We have some savings but not enough to last more than a few months."

"I don't have any savings," Karrie said. "Mom and I live paycheck to paycheck. Rent in San Diego isn't cheap, you know."

"I do know," Cindy said. "I hope I don't have to visit the food banks again."

"You've had to visit those too?"

"Yeah," Cindy sighed. "I've had hard times since I've been married too. Doesn't it seem like the cards are stacked against some people?" She turned on her wipers as the rain came down harder.

"It does." Karrie looked into the dark, wet night.

"Did you ever tell your mom that you were changing majors to get a traditional liberal arts degree? How did that go?"

"Not well. Mom wants me to get a good job now. She thinks I'll just flunk out and I owe a lot in student loans. We ended up arguing about my dad coming home. It got really ugly."

"That's kind of harsh. Is your dad getting out?"

"Yes, the average convictions for child molestation are only three years. Can you believe that?"

"And the survivor has to live with the scares their whole life," Cindy said through gritted teeth.

"Exactly. My dad has served five years, and she wants to see him again." She stared at the rain pounding on the windshield. "She yelled at me for not forgiving him and then for changing my major."

"I don't think you're going to flunk out of college. You should try to get what you want in life. Although..." Cindy sighed as she pulled in front of Karrie's apartment complex.

"The world is changing. Who knows what the future holds for anyone of us."

Karrie shrugged.

"Boy, your place is all lit up," Cindy said as Karrie opened the door. "I wonder if your mom has company."

"I hope not," Karrie whispered.

Cindy grabbed her arm as she started to get out of the car. "Have you thought about accepting Isabella's invitation to live in her house?"

"Not lately. She made that offer a year ago, and I'm not sure if it's still open."

"Think about it," Cindy said as she pulled away from the curb.

Karrie walked cautiously toward the front door. The last time she had heard music like that coming out of her house was when her father was home. A pit of fear grew in her stomach.

She opened the front door, and the smell of marijuana hit her in the face. Beer cans covered the dining room table. Her father and mother sat on the living room couch.

"Welcome home, working girl," her mother slurred. "It's my little working girl." She got up from the sofa to kiss Karrie on the cheek. Her mom reeked of alcohol.

"Mom, what's he doing here?" Karrie backed up to be closer to the doorway.

"Don't worry. It's just a visit."

"Is he going to stay the night?" she whispered.

"Now, little girl, I don't think that's any of your business," her mother laughed.

"Don't worry, Karrie. I'm not going to touch you," her father sneered at her. "I learned my lesson. Five years was long enough for me."

"You're supposed to stay away from me." Karrie stuck out her chin so her father wouldn't see her bottom lip quiver.

"Until you were eighteen. Now you're nineteen, and I told you. I ain't gonna touch you."

"I'm not staying here if he's staying." Karrie pushed her mother aside and headed toward her room.

"You're being ridiculous." Her mother followed her into her room. "You're the one who claims to be such a good Christian, and Christians are supposed to forgive and forget. Right?"

Karrie shook her head and rolled her eyes. She pulled out her backpack and stuffed it with clothing.

"Is this Christian love? Huh, Karrie? You're the great Christian woman running out in bitterness. Bitterness is a sin! I'm so tired of you judging me! That's all you've ever done is judge us!"

Karrie looked frantically around the room to see if she had left anything important. When she turned around, her father was standing by her mother.

"Now, just what are you frightened of little girl? What in the Sam Hill do you think I'm gonna do to you?"

Karrie opened her mouth to speak, but no words came out. She looked at her mother, who was on the verge of tears. Why couldn't Karrie speak? She ran around her father and bolted out the front door.

"Don't bother going after her," her father said. "She'll be back. After all, where is she gonna go?"

Karrie ran to University Avenue to the nearest bus stop. When she got there, she pulled out her phone and texted Isabella.

<can I come over? I had a blow up with my mother, and I need a place to stay tonight>

<Sure, you, okay?>

<yes, just need a place>

<you got one>

<I'll text you when I get there>

<good>

The bus creaked up beside her and heaved a mechanical sigh as its doors opened. Karrie reached into her backpack to find her wallet and realized it wasn't there. It must have fallen out of her backpack as she was packing.

She waved the bus pass and started to walk down the street. A couple of men sharing a bottle of wine on a corner hooted and hollered, yelling obscenities at her. She pulled up her collar and wrapped her scarf tighter around her face as she walked east as fast as she could. Soon she'd be at Thirtieth and University, where all the trendy coffee shops were. She'd be safe there.

She quickened her pace. When she arrived at the corner of Thirtieth Street, she stopped to adjust her scarf and wipe the tangled wet hair off of her face. A car pulled out in front of her. A group of fashionable college girls climbed out, fluffing their hair, and laughing.

"Nice hair, girl." One girl laughed while looking at Karrie as they passed by.

If she knew where I've come from or what I've been through, maybe she wouldn't turn her nose up at me. Karrie turned up Thirtieth toward El Cajon Boulevard. *Or maybe she would.*

Lo'laini said paper-thin people were everywhere, so don't let them cut you with their sharp edges. Those people didn't seem to bother Lo'laini, but they did bother Karrie. Those paper-thin people had left horrific cuts on her for her entire life.

Soon Karrie was on El Cajon Boulevard. Apartments and family restaurants lined the street. She felt safer there. When she reached Fifty-Fourth and El Cajon, a young family crossed the street. Her heart ached when their toddler dropped his ice cream cone. The Mother cleaned him off while the father made funny faces to stop the little boy from crying.

She kept walking until she reached College Avenue. "Almost there," she said to herself as she turned toward San Diego State University, a car pulled up beside her. A couple of drunk college boys made crass remarks.

"Great. High-class winos and predators," she thought as she passed San Diego State and crossed the bridge into Del Cerro. A few blocks later, she finally reached Isabella's house. Karrie pulled out her phone.

<OK, I @ the door>

<On my way>

Karrie put her phone back into her backpack. She pulled off her knitted scarf and wrung out the rainwater, splattering it on the porch. The porch light turned on, the door opened, and a rush of relief passed over Karrie when she saw Isabella's face.

"Oh, you look like a drowned rat. You look like you're chilled to the bone. Did you walk all the way from North Park?"

Karrie nodded.

"Okay, inside," Isabella commanded, and Karrie willingly obeyed. "I wish I could hug you, but you know Covid restrictions. I have a terrycloth bathrobe that I just took out of the dryer. Strip down, and we'll talk over some hot chocolate."

Isabella's house smelled like cinnamon and apples, and it was warm. Karrie made her way to the bathroom, where she stripped down and wrung out her clothes in the bathtub. She wrapped herself in the robe and shyly walked to the kitchen. Isabella sat at the table reading a tattered notebook while wiping away tears.

"I'm so sorry to come tonight. I heard about your mom's death," Karrie said as she sat at the table. "Maybe I shouldn't have come."

"Of course, you should've." Isabella poured hot chocolate from an electric tea pot in the center of the table. "I invited you to live here. I'm glad you finally decided to take me up on my offer. I always feared for your safety at your mother's house."

Karrie wrapped her shivering hands around the cup of hot chocolate and held it to her chin. Chocolate-scented stream engulfed her face, soothing her chilled nose and trembling lips.

"I called the funeral home to arrange Mom's funeral. Because of the pandemic, we're going to Zoom the service."

"An online funeral sounds difficult."

"Not really. In some ways, it will give us more privacy, especially since we have a two-year-old and an infant." Isabella picked up the tattered notebook she'd been reading when Karrie walked in. "I found this while cleaning the small house. Mom lived there after my stepfather, Jose, died and after she received the cancer diagnosis. In her last days, she wrote about her journey from Guatemala to California."

Isabella sighed as she thumbed through the tattered pages. "Before Mama died, she wanted to talk about a fight we had during my first year of college. I wanted to listen to her but thought there would be more time. I thought she was getting better, and I was thinking of ways to get her home so we could talk here. Then Alejandro called, and I had to leave the room. When I came back, she was gone." Isabella reached for a tissue to wipe her eyes.

"I'm sure she knew you loved her."

"I am too. I just hate that mom felt so unsettled about that fight. I called her a coward. I called my mother—who fled from the Guatemalan civil war with a child on her back and walked all the way to the Arizona/Mexican border—a coward. I'd forgotten all about that fight and those stupid, cruel words, but she didn't. She wrote about it in this notebook, and she described her horrific journey to this country."

"I can't imagine you calling anyone a coward. Are you sure you remembered it correctly? Why would you call her a coward?"

"I remember it. I was a stupid, arrogant kid who'd taken her first class in the psychology of ethnicity." Isabella closed the notebook. "When I was kid, I thought my stepfather was my biological dad. He was an engineer when she and Mom met at church. I knew he loved my mom and me, and Mom was kind to him, but I could tell something was missing between them and I resented it. I tried to bring them closer together by making these romantic dinners and trying to force my mom to tell my stepfather that she loved him. In junior high, my stepfather told me to stop interfering with them. He told me I was getting too involved in adult matters that were private things between him and my mom. I grudgingly stopped, but I felt like my mom was cheating my stepfather out of love and romance.

"When I went to college, I started getting chest pains, so I went to the student clinics. They asked about my family history. I told them my parents didn't have any health problems, but I didn't know anything about my extended family history because they were both immigrants. The doctor gave me a number and asked if my mother could call them with the family history. One afternoon, I came home from school early and heard my mom on the phone. She said my father often got chest pains and she thought it was asthma. It was never diagnosed because they'd never seen a doctor because they were farm workers in Guatemala. That was the first time I'd heard that we weren't Mexican and Jose wasn't my father. I could hear an affection in my mom's voice when she talked about my biological father which she never showed to Jose, and it angered me. I was even more angry that Mom lied to me all those years. I burst into the room and yelled, 'No wonder you've never loved Dad!' I disarmed her with my anger. She hung up the phone as I continued ranting. I yelled, 'Don't deny it! You've never loved Dad! All this time you've been lying about our lives! You made me believe a lie about myself and where I came from!" Isabella rolled her eyes and sat back in her chair. "I thought I was defending my dad, but I was being hurtful. I yelled about things I didn't know about. When she tried to explain that some things were too difficult for her to share with me, I screamed back. 'That's what you always do. You clam up when things are hard to talk about!' Then I called her a coward."

Isabella looked at the tattered notebook in exasperation and said, "I called my mom, who risked her life carrying me on her back through the desert, a coward. My dad came home later that night and talked with me. He told me things happened to immigrants as they traveled through the desert to get to this country—things I didn't know about that he prayed I would never know about, and I was never to talk to my mom that way again. I apologized to Mom. She tried to tell me about my biological father, but I didn't want to hear it. It felt like I was betraying my stepdad, who I thought was my real dad. Three years before Mom descended into dementia, she tried to tell me about him, but I was too busy to listen. She tried to tell me again right before she died, and I still didn't listen."

Karrie waited some time before she said, "I'm sorry, Isabella."

"I got a chance to listen today while I was cleaning out her things." Isabella picked up the notebook. "And my mom was no coward. She was courageous. She gave up everything to protect me. I don't remember when I felt unprotected or unsafe, and I never knew what it cost her to make me safe until I read this."

"I envy you." Karrie took a drink of hot chocolate. "You've had people you could depend on who wanted to protect you. Sometimes my mom tried to protect me, but she's so changeable when my dad's around."

"I'm so sorry, Karrie. You sure looked frightened when I opened the door. Are you okay? I was so wrapped up in this diary that I didn't think to ask how you're doing. What made you finally decide to leave?"

"I'm okay, even having to walk nine miles after five hours of work and three hours of school. Not that I'm complaining about the work hours. You know I need my hours. Estella gave us the news today about the restaurant closing. I know you'll be cutting staff. I'm kind of hoping I can keep my hours."

"We haven't made those decisions yet. For now, let's worry about today. What happened that made you walk nine miles in the rain to get here?"

"I came home, and my mom and dad were sitting on the couch together. I knew he was moving back in again, which meant my whole world would be chaotic again. But I didn't cry this time. I just got angry, and it felt good to get angry."

"Anger is not always bad if it helps us make the right decisions," Isabella said.

"That's what Pastor Lydia told me. When I was leaving my mom's house, my dad asked what I was frightened of, and I couldn't answer. I opened my mouth, but no words came out. I saw my mom, and I knew if I said anything, she would cry. I didn't want to comfort her this time, so I left with them screaming after me."

"You don't have to explain to me."

"But I want to tell you because I learned something, and if I talk about it now, I'll remember it better. It's not that I think my mom doesn't love me—she can behave very lovingly toward me—but she's never known how to keep me safe, not when it comes to the men in her life. She can be cruel when my dad or brothers turn on me. Tonight, I learned that not only hasn't she been protecting me, but I've been protecting her. Ever since I was a little girl, I've protected her. People say all you need is love, but I know that I need more. I need..."

"Safety?" Isabella asked.

"More than safety. I need respect," Karrie said. "To feel at home, you've got to be able to let your guard down. To let your guard down, you have to have a minimal amount of respect. Someone can't protect you if they don't respect you.

"You felt loved because your mom thought about your feelings. My mom isn't capable of thinking about my feelings where my dad is concerned."

"Trust starts with safety and respect. Maybe while you're here, you can create a space where you feel safe and respected," Isabella reached over and took Karrie's hand.

Karrie nodded.

†

Chapter Seventeen

The Fragility of Familiarity

Lo'laini's Family

Lo'laini's chest throbbed as she slammed the front door behind her and ran down the street, her bare feet slapping against the rain-soaked pavement. Tears streamed down her face.

How could a simple conversation go so wrong? The angry words that bubbled to the surface poisoned the visit Lo'laini had planned so carefully. Why did things always have to fall apart? Anger was an interfering guest at every family gathering she could remember. When would the screams of unresolved family conflicts stop following her?

A week earlier, Lo'laini's heart had burst with joy when she saw her grandmother descending the airport escalator ten days earlier. Tutu looked so bright in the new pink suit Lo'laini had given her. Tutu's hair was pinned in an elegant French bun.

Lo'laini had emailed Tutu a link for professional hairstyles. She wanted to show her aunts the more sophisticated side of her grandmother. Tutu complied, although somewhat disapprovingly.

"Don't paint me white," Aninki said months earlier in a late-night telephone conversation. "That color will not suit me well."

"No, Tutu. I am not doing that," Lo'laini said. "I want to show them what a professional woman you are."

"With an overpriced suit? I would think my financial portfolio was a better indicator of my professionalism than an overpriced English suit. Mo 'opuna, I can find overpriced clothing in Hawaii. I own a shop that takes advantage of tourists with these kinds of frivolous purchases."

"But I want to dress you for this trip. Please, Tutu."

"Do you like it in the UK working in Aunt Sandra's business?" her grandmother asked.

"For now," Lo'laini said. "Everybody treats me well. But I miss you. I miss you so much."

"I'll be there shortly,"

At Heathrow Airport, Tutu descended the escalator with the perfect picture of the professional woman Lo'laini wanted to present to her aunts. She nudged Aunt Sandra.

Sandra nodded and smiled. "Quite a transformation, indeed."

"If it were necessary," Emily sighed.

"I am just trying to support Lo'laini in her creativity and efforts," Sandra whispered to Emily.

"I don't want Aninki to think she has to dress up for us. It's not as if we walk around looking like the Duke and Duchess of Sussex."

"Still, one does like to make a proper effort." Sandra took off her sunglasses and smoothed her scarf.

Lo'laini's face brightened when she saw Tutu. Lo'laini pushed her way through the crowd and lunged into her grandmother's embrace. Her aunts followed with warm smiles and an offer to help carry Tutu's carry-on bags.

"Wait a moment." Tutu smiled as she opened one of her bags and presented two orchid leis to Sandra and Emily. Lo'laini looked nervously around at the people turning their heads to watch as Tutu placed each of the leis around her aunt's neck. Lo'laini's face flushed as travelers smiled at her gifts.

"I am sorry," Tutu said. "They're slightly browned from being jostled in transit."

"The best gifts are those that have been tattered a little by life," Aunt Emily said, moving forward to embrace her.

When Aninki placed the final lei around Lo'laini's neck, she whispered into her ear, "Mo 'opuna, are you embarrassed by my hospitality? I hope you haven't become too sophisticated for your Tutu."

"No, Tutu," Lo'laini said, wiping away a tear. "It's so good to see you."

"Nothing to be embarrassed about," Aunt Sandra said. "We are quite international here in the UK, surely."

"We've planned to take you to the best tea house, the theater, and then a rose garden." Lo'laini whipped out her phone and showed Tutu the places on her agenda.

"All in one afternoon?" She laughed while placing her arm around Lo'laini.

"No, over the next three days," Emily smiled. "Meanwhile, let's get your baggage and get you home so you can freshen up."

The next three days were filled with delicious noontime teas, museums, musical theater, and late-night walks and talks sprinkled with laughter and family jokes. Lo'laini beamed with pride while hearing Aunt Sandra and Tutu discuss the effect of the trade wars on their merchandise and the tourist trade. Her heart warmed as she watched Aninki teach Aunt Emily how to cook roast pork over steamed rice.

Lo'laini fell asleep smiling each night, feeling she had finally brought peace into her world. The memory of her father screaming at Tutu while her mother was dying still stung like a dagger in her chest. "I don't want my daughter anywhere near those women!" he'd said. His voice echoed in her ears from Christmases when her mother tried to reach out to her aunts. "There will be no more screaming," she said to herself as she drifted off to sleep. "I think I've solved everything now."

The following day, while Lo'laini helped Tutu pack her new souvenirs in her carry-on. "Why does luggage always shrink on the return voyage?" Tutu laughed as Lo'laini sat on the overstuffed old bag, bouncing up down trying to shut it.

As she bounced, someone knocked on the guest room door. Aunt Emily entered the room with Sandra behind her. Emily's face was pale, and she was trembling. Sandra stood soberly behind her. Lo'laini and her grandmother stopped laughing.

"What's wrong?" Tutu asked, rising from her bed to make room for Emily to sit.

"I'm okay, which is odd. I feel fine. I'm not sick. But I received notification today ..." Emily's voice tapered off as she choked back tears.

Aunt Sandra placed her hand on Emily's back. "She received word today that she has been diagnosed with the coronavirus."

"Are up okay, Aunt Emily?"

"Completely, I do not feel a thing. That's the oddness of all this. And I'm sorry, Aninki, but we all must quarantine for fourteen days. We'll have to cancel your flight."

"I'll contact my employees tonight. They can watch the shop. I hope my staying here longer won't be too much of an inconvenience." Tutu pulled out her phone to call her shop.

"You may have to close your shop altogether. Many government officials are calling for a shutdown of all public shops and businesses," Sandra said, showing her the article on her phone that listed all the businesses that closed in London that morning.

"It can't be that drastic. A shutdown of all commerce?" Tutu frowned and fumbled with her phone, searching all the closed businesses in Hawaii.

"Are you sure that you are well?" Aunt Sandra asked. "This isn't the time to play brave little soldier."

"Yes, I'm quite well. Just wondering how we shall do cooped up in our little cottage for fourteen days," Emily said.

"We've had fun thus far, haven't we?" Sandra opened the window beside her. "We'll keep the windows open. Fresh air and exercise—that's the ticket. We'll be one happy family."

But they weren't as happy as Sandra predicted. Just as Aninki's suitcase shanked under the weight of too many keepsakes, so the shared spaces shrank in the back cottage as all four women settled in for the next fourteen days. The cottage seemed overloaded, with them cautiously avoiding each other throughout the house. Phrases such as *Excuse me,* and *I beg your pardon*—that had previously not been necessary—

became necessary by words whenever two or more people passed in the hallway or shared the kitchen.

Subtle signs of disapproval about housekeeping surfaced. The first time Lo'laini noticed was after Aunt Emily cleaned up after baking apple muffins for breakfast. Tutu causally entered the kitchen and swept the floor a second time. After that, Aunt Sandra came in and inspected the floor before sweeping it a third time.

Aunt Emily chuckled at the competition between Tutu and Aunt Sandra. As a practical joke, she started leaving one thing undone when she finished cleaning up to see how quickly both women would return and try to outdo each other with their household standards.

One morning, she cleaned the kitchen after making scones, leaving out one spatula. She nestled into her window seat when Tutu came in, put away the spatula, and wiped the counters a second time. Then Aunt Sandra followed by wiping the counters and sweeping the floor a third time. Tutu showed no pretense of ignoring Aunt Sandra's third cleaning but staring at her over her knitting. Aunt Emily impishly looked up from her book and caught Lo'laini's eye, making Lo'laini's body shake with restrained laughter.

"Is it my turn to clean now?" Lo'laini whispered to Aunt Emily.

"Don't you dare move a muscle?" Tiny tears of restrained laughter ran down Emily's face as she wrestled with muting her explosion of merriment.

There were other minor household infractions, such as pillows not fluffed properly, food rejected with an upturned nose, or dishes being re-seasoned after placing them on the table. But the animosity between the matriarchs painfully surfaced when Lo'laini mentioned taking a mission trip the next summer.

After dinner, Lo'laini, Aunt Emily, and Tutu lingered at the table long after Aunt Sandra excused herself to go work in her office. Lo'laini turned over some pale white noodles with her fork, bathing them repeatedly in the brown sauce from the beef stroganoff.

Aunt Emily opened the window to let the golden rays of sunlight pour into the room. "Now, there's a sunset to behold."

"Whatever happened to your friend Karrie?" Tutu asked, getting up from the table to search for her knitting needles. "Do you two still keep in touch?"

"She still emails me. Texting is too expensive over here." Lo'laini finally pushed her plate away, finished with torturing the final noodles she had no intention of eating. "She lives with Isabella now, which is closer to her school."

"She moved out of the mother's house?" Tutu settled down in one of the overstuffed chairs.

"Yeah. I guess it was a good move." Lo'laini got up and started to clear the table.

Tutu nodded.

"Karrie's going on a mission trip next summer with her church, which used to be my church."

"That must be exciting," Emily said, wiping down the table after Lo'laini had put away the dishes.

"But with this pandemic, things might change." Lo'laini squeezed out a sponge in the sink then wiped the counters.

"Things have changed, indeed," Sandra said, coming in from the office to give her final inspection. "It seems an archaic business to me, mission trips. Isn't that a practice left over from imperial colonial days?"

"I don't know, Sandra." Emily stirred the embers in the fireplace into flames. "If you're talking about feeding the hungry and clothing the naked, those seem like pretty timeless themes."

"Yes, but don't you think commerce would do a better job raising people's living standards? As the adage goes, give a man a fish and he'll eat for a day, but teach him to fish and he'll eat for a lifetime. There are reasons corny statements like that pass the test of time."

"Perhaps if businesspeople could organize themselves and move beyond their greed and self-interests," Emily poked the smoldering log, "it would do a better job of helping people."

"Rather derogatory remark for you to make about business, Emily. Especially since you profit from our family business."

Emily shrugged while she continued to stir flames.

"You might be surprised," Aunt Sandra said. "Compassionate giving has become quite fashionable in some corners. It has even become a very lucrative business."

"Until something as unfortunate as a pandemic puts us all out of business." Emily dusted off her hands and replaced the fire screen before snuggling into the soft pillows she kept by the fireplace.

"In such insurmountable cases, we must rely on a higher power who transcends our difficulties," Tutu said, looking up from her knitting to look at Aunt Sandra "Isn't God the one who calls us into missions in the first place?"

"Divine calls inspire some people, but some of us are called by our consciences and common-sense calls others," Sandra said.

"Actually, Aunt Sandra, I've been thinking about going on a mission trip next summer."

"Really? That might be a worthy goal for you in a year or two after settling down and knowing what career you want to pursue, but such trips can be very emotional, so don't get too carried away. I wouldn't want you to throw your professional life away on a lost cause."

Tutu wrinkled her forehead. "What do you mean getting carried away on a lost cause?"

"Aunt Emily, my head hurts. Do we still have some aspirin?" Lo'laini put down her sponge to rub her forehead.

"Yes, dear. In the cabinet in the loo."

As Lo'laini walked down the hall to get some medicine, she could hear the adults' voices behind her.

"I am sorry, Aninki. I meant no offense, but you know we had a history with our brother. I think his fanatical faith was the beginning of his end."

"That's hardly fair, Sandra," Aunt Emily said. "He was using drugs long before he professed Christianity."

Lo'laini's face felt hot, and her head throbbed. After she reached the bathroom, she turned on the faucet and splashed cold water against her face, partly to cool her face and partly to drown out the voices from the living room.

"He had a beautiful faith when he first met Mai," Tutu said.

"Okay," Sandra laughed. "I'm the doubting Thomas here, outnumbered by the true believers. I humbly apologize for my criticism and doubt."

"No one is asking you to apologize for your convictions, Sandra. We just don't want you to belittle ours." Emily got up from her pile of pillows as Lo'laini reentered the room.

"Why do you guys always do this?" Lo'laini asked, breathless and leaning up against the door frame.

"Lo'laini, you don't look well. Are you okay?" Tutu set down her knitting and moved toward Lo'laini, but she held up her hand to stop her from coming closer.

"What do you think we are doing, dear?" Emily asked.

"Talking about my dad. Whenever I talk about something I want to do, you bring up my dad and his faith. You don't know anything about my dad's faith." She gasped as she swayed backward.

"You really don't look good, dear." Aunt Sandra pulled out a chair. "Perhaps you should sit down and let us take your temperature."

"Tutu, whenever they talk about Dad, you bring up Mom." Lo'laini swooned again but steadied herself against the wall. "It's as if you're saying the only good thing about Dad was Mom, which isn't true. Mom and Dad were both Christians. They were different, but they were both," she gasped again for air. "Good people."

"Look at us. No one is arguing now." Emily moved toward Lo'laini. "We weren't really arguing when you were in the loo. We were rather joking, teasing each other about our differences. That's what people who love each other do. Now sit down so we can take your temperature. You look ill."

"No! I'm not sitting down. My back and legs hurt. I've got to get out of this house!"

Before anyone could step in front of her, Lo'laini bolted through the front door and ran down the sidewalk. She could hear them calling behind her, but she ran until she stopped in the cool rain, shaking and chilling. Then, she heard a familiar voice call out her name.

"Luni, girl, what are you doing?"

"Dad?" She looked up. Her father stood in front of her, wearing a white tea shirt and cutoff jeans. His hair was matted and wet, like when he took her surfing. "What are you doing here?"

"You shouldn't be in the rain when you're ill. Get back to the house so your grandmother and aunts can care for you."

"You don't like my aunts and you yelled at my grandma." Lo'laini squinted through the rain as her father's image changed from sober to drunk.

"I was wrong, Luni. Now, let's get you home."

"You keep phasing in and out. It's hard to see you. No! You're not here. You died! You left me in that car accident. I saw you go through the windshield. No, no. You're not here!"

"Oh, Danny. Thank God, you found her. Everyone was so worried."

A shadowy figure moved toward Lo'laini. As it came closer, she recognized her mother's voice. "Young lady, what do you mean talking back to your aunts and grandmother that way? Come on. Let's get you back to that house."

"No, this isn't real. You're gone. Cancer took you away. It hurt so bad when you left."

"I'm here now. Let's start walking home, where you'll be safe. You that I am always with you, you carry on piece of me."

"Why are you here? Why now?"

"To help you find a forgotten door you once called home."

"Come on, kid."

Lo'laini's father's warm hand covered hers. "Let's start the long walk home."

When Lo'laini entered the door, someone wrapped her in a warm blanket while someone else placed a thermometer on her throbbing head.

"No! Stop tugging on me! Stop pulling me apart," Lo'laini said as firm hands pushed her down on couch.

"What did she say?"

Lo'laini turned her head, and her father's face melted into Aunt Emily's face.

"I don't know. I think she's delirious," Sandra said. "The ambulance will be here in five minutes."

"Not soon enough," Tutu said as she wrapped the blanket tighter around her. Her mother's image faded into Tutu's concerned gaze.

Chapter Eighteen

Sandra Struggle

The Weight of Ancestry

The Larks Gale estate family chapel sat between the servants' quarters and the kitchen, which placed it in the shadow of the grand estate. Townspeople often remarked the chapel looked as if the family was trying to hide it from the public as one might try to hide an awkward relative. The brass plate on the chapel door read *In Honor of Our Faithful Servants.* As soon as the chapel was built, rumors and innuendos surfaced about why it had been made.

The plain exterior of the simple stone chapel supplied the family with a sanctuary, prayer books, and Bibles placed in twelve neat pews covered in red velvet. The fabric had become tattered and faded with time. Seven stained glass windows chronicled Christ's journey to Calvary through the stations of the cross. At sunset, light streamed through the windows and illuminated five tapestries depicting Christ's miracles. The tapestries portrayed household servants as recipients of Christ's miracles.

The first tapestry portrayed Jesus healing the son of the widow of Nain from Luke seven. The widow appeared as a field hand peering over Jesus's shoulder as he touched her son. The next tapestry showed the woman with chronic bleeding from Matthew nine as a scullery maid reaching up from scrubbing a floor to touch the hem of Jesus's garment. The next image reimagined the Canaanite woman from Mark seven as a Nanny interrupting a fine dinner to talk to Jesus, much to the horror of the lords and dukes in attendance. The last tapestry was of Mary Magdalene from Luke ten as a housekeeper listening to Jesus by the fire while the resentful Martha—a harried cook—looked longingly from the kitchen door into the comfortable room where Jesus and Mary conversed by the fireside.

Local gossip suggested the servants in the tapestries confirmed a rumor that the chapel had been built in honor of a scullery maid who died giving birth to a child who looked suspiciously like the master of the house. The family's lore was that the family built the chapel in honor of a nanny who died after nursing the children through the smallpox epidemic. Time erased the possibility of discovering the true motivation for the portrayal of the servants in the tapestries, but over the years, the chapel became a place of refuge for grieving townspeople.

Grieving mothers and wives had fled there in the shadow of the slaughter of World War I to share each other's grief. Nurses and doctors found refuge there during the influenza outbreak in 1917 when the estate housed an overflow of patients. Shaken parishioners from Germany's heartless blitzes met there when bombs decimated their own churches during World War II.

The family never allowed the chapel to be locked during wars, so people could be found sitting quietly in pews and sometimes gazing at the tapestries at all hours of the day.

By the time Sandra took over the estate, the chapel had been boarded up and fallen into disrepair. The kitchen and chapel were the first two renovations she ordered as she prepared the estate to become a venue for weddings and social gatherings.

During the chapel's construction, one of the workers told Sandra about a ministry looking for a space to rent for services. Sandra offered the chapel to the fellowship rent-free, agreeing they would leave the chapel free every Friday evening and all-day Saturday for weddings. She agreed to pay all building costs, such as plumbing and masonry work, but they were responsible for any indoor renovations they wanted to make.

She suspected they would want to make a good number of changes to the interior.

Sandra's hunch had paid off. In the first year the congregation took residence in the chapel, they had central heating, a new sound system, and new cloth coverings for the pews. They painted the chapel's entrance and laid new tile in the back vestry to create a nursery and playroom for small children.

"Very good, Sandra," Emily said one evening after clearing the table. "You managed to get free improvements on your property while also being seen as a great philanthropist."

"You needn't be so cynical. The deal was not completely one-sided" Sandra got up from the table. "They need a place for their worship service, and an empty building is a hazard. I'm glad for their occupation, and they're glad for the space. It's a win for both for us."

When the pandemic hit, they had to close the chapel except for family use. Aninki used it every morning for prayer, and eventually, Lo'laini joined her. Occasionally, Emily joined them and read scripture, sang, and prayed.

The morning after Lo'laini's illness, Sandra sat alone in the chapel in a stream of blue-tinted sunlight that ran through the eighth station of the cross window which reflected on the tapestry of the scullery maid reaching up to touch the hem of Jesus's garment.

The tapestry captured her attention as a young girl when she sat fidgeting during her cousin's christening. As a teenager, it made Sandra giggle when a friend revealed the rumors about the tapestry.

After the day's trauma, however, the picture invoked an attitude of reverence as the beautiful scullery maid tried to grasp something out of her reach. The events of the last few years swam in her mind like an unsolved math equation that would not let her rest until she found the solution. She recounted each event that pulled on her heartstrings: negotiating Lo'laini's custody with Aninki, Daniel's unexpected but predictable death, Daniel's funeral, Lo'laini's refreshing presence in their lives, Lo'laini eagerly following her throughout each business day as an ambitious prodigy.

All those images culminated with the memory of Aninki and Emily trying to lead Lo'laini back to the house. Sandra remembered calling for an ambulance while fumbling through the kitchen drawer for a thermometer. Still, on the phone, she placed it against Lo'laini's head while Emily and Aninki tried to keep her still on the sofa. Sandra's heart broke when Lo'laini cried, "You're tearing me apart!"

When the ambulance arrived, Sandra opened the door to three workers dressed in protective gear. As they approached the sofa, Lo'laini cringed in a feverish delirium. Emily and Aninki coaxed Lo'laini into the ambulance. At the same time,

Sandra answered questions about Lo'laini's contacts for the last month and listened to further instructions about quarantine.

After Sandra posted the instructions on the kitchen bulletin board, she returned to the living room and saw that Lo'laini was already gone. Emily curled up on the sofa, softly weeping, while Aninki stoically looked out the window. Sandra was numb. She gathered up the hospital papers she'd signed, walked to her office desk, and locked them away.

"Come join us by the fire, Sandi." Emily sobbed.

"Sandi? You haven't called me that since we were girls." Sandra half smiled while looking at a stack of papers on her desk. "Don't you think we've been rather stupid and conceited these last few days?"

"Excuse me? What are you saying?"

"We all sat in front of the telly and watched the infected and dead numbers rise. The death toll grew from half a million to one million without us shedding one tear. Our investments have preoccupied me." Sandra's face flushed, and she bit her lip to hold back tears. "Numbers. During all this death, that's what I've been worried about. Then, when it's someone we love, someone whose face we know, we fall apart. Isn't that the definition of selfishness?"

"Yes, I suppose," Emily said. "But I cannot look at things the way you do. I don't have the same kind of logic and reason you always employ. I cannot solve the world's problems. I'm saddened by the people who've died during this pandemic and personally hurt by being separated from my students. But at this moment, I only have enough emotional room in my world for the people I love."

"I'll join you later this evening." Sandra's trembling hands picked up a stack of papers. "I have a few tasks I need to get done today."

"Please, Sandra. Please join us now. Aninki has called Lo'laini's pastor to pray with us. I want you to join us for one prayer." Emily's voice broke as she started to weep again. "I don't care if you fake it. I don't care if don't believe it. I just need you there as my sister. Please join us."

"I will later today." Sandra heaved a sigh. "You really think I don't believe, Emily?" She swallowed hard to fight back her tears.

"I believe, I've never stopped believing. It's not that I don't have faith, it's that I'm tormented by my faith. I am tormented by the searing disappointment I feel when God allows pain in this world and all this suffering that slips through His fingers. I still have the faith that we had as children, the faith formed during our confirmation class, lived out at the vicarage, and nurtured in our stone chapel at family gatherings. The problem is it hurts too much to pray again because I've prayed so many times before and..." her voice broke into sobs. "I lost the people I loved. It won't do this time, my sister. It simply won't do!" Sandra pushed Emily out of the way and bolted through the back door.

Emily started to follow, but Aninki stopped her and whispered, "Don't. Look where she's heading. She's running toward the family chapel."

As Sandra pushed through the heavy wooden doors, the colors streaming through the windows quieted and calmed her. She entered the chapel under the pretense of checking for mouse droppings and water damage from the last storm, but the rainbow-hued light captivated her.

The stack of papers fell from her hands and scattered across the floor. She looked for her childhood seat: the eighth pew under the tapestry of the woman with chronic bleeding.

As the colors faded and evening engulfed the chapel in darkness, Sandra stayed. Something inside her refused to let her get up. The door creaked behind her, and she knew she had company. She could hear the steps of Emily and Aninki, who stood in the door frame.

"Has the hospital called?" she asked without turning around. "What treatment are they giving her?"

"They're working at getting the fever down," Emily said as she turned on the lights.

"Her breathing is fine for now. With Covid, breath is the number one concern," Aninki said as she and Emily walked down the aisle and sat beside Sandra.

She kept her gaze on the tapestry. "What hypocrites our ancestors were when they built this chapel."

"I see no hypocrisy." Emily gazed at the tapestries. "This chapel has been loved by this community."

"They built a chapel in memorial for a servant, then used servants' images as in these biblical stories while paying those same servants starvation wages. It's unforgivable."

"Isn't forgiveness the lessons of these bible stories? They could have and should have done better, but all of us should do better." Emily reached over to take Sandra's hand.

All three women sat in silence, gazing at the tapestry until Aninki spoke.

"Sandra, you once asked me a question when we were planning Daniel's funeral that I think I would like to answer now. You asked if it made me angry that the descendants of missionaries exploited my people and our lands."

"Was I that insensitive?" Sandra rolled her eyes at the memory.

Aninki nodded. "You were that direct."

"I am so sorry," she whispered.

"I want you to know that I do get angry. The dearest force in my life is Jesus Christ, so I feel betrayed when I hear stories of what happened to my ancestors. My grandmother went to a missionary school, where they used to prick her tongue with a pin if she spoke our native language. That story still haunts me.

"The people who brought the gospel to my family were flawed, but God's love was a great light in our lives. I can't make sense of those contradictions. I still get angry when tourists speak to me in a condescending or entitled manner, and I was angry when you suggested Lo'laini might do better in your custody as opposed to mine."

Emily gasped, but before she could say anything, Aninki laid her hand on Emily's knee and continued. "Please let me finish. Lo'laini is here because she wants to be here, but I've been praying for the courage to tell you that what I have to teach her about her Hawaiian culture is as important as her English culture and your family estate."

"Without a doubt." Emily embraced Aninki.

"Sandra, I also want to say that as a person whose family has seen oppression, I don't only see the oppression of classism and bigotry in these tapestries. I also see the people Christ chooses to minister to. I see how Christ's love surpasses that oppression. Christ's presence is always in the empowerment and healing of the oppressed. He is not in oppression, but He is in the healing of the oppressed. These tapestries may have been made out of guilt, but they surpass their original purpose by showing that Christ's healing is accessible to everyone."

"And they have become a powerful shelter for people caught in the storms of life," Emily said.

Sandra nodded.

"All my life, I have stared at this tapestry," Sandra whispered. "But I never realized how vulnerable and alone that scullery maid must have felt."

"The woman in the bible or the women who people say died in childbirth because of our ancestor?" Emily softy asked.

"I guess both," Sandra answered.

"I can't speak to servant, but I know that the hemorrhaging women in scripture, was indeed, vulnerable. Aninki said, walking over to the tapestry. "I think this tapestry is a beautiful portrayal of Jesus's compassion toward vulnerable people."

"But why did Jesus have to call her out?" Sandra asked, rubbing her forehead. "That's what he did in the story, right? He asked *who touched me,* then everyone saw who she was. Why couldn't he heal her in silence? Let her have anonymity."

"I suppose, from a theological point, it was an opportunity for the woman to make a public confession," Aninki said. "Confession is the hallmark of Christianity. Our faith begins when we name Jesus as lord, and our sanctification continues as we voice our reliance on him."

Sandra heaved another sigh. "A very good theological answer." She reached out and took her sister's hand. "I'm sorry I yelled at you this afternoon and didn't join you for prayer."

Emily kissed Sandra's hand, then rested her head on her sister's shoulder. Aninki put her hand on theirs.

"Personally, I believe Jesus wanted to give her a voice because of the kind bleeding she had," Aninki said. "A minister once told me the Greek word that describes her kind of bleeding translates to *a flow*."

"You mean menstruation?" gasped Emily. "They speak of menstruation in the bible?"

Aninki nodded.

"And for seven years!" Sandra let out an exasperated laugh. "Suddenly, I understand what the text means when it says she suffered at the hands of many doctors. I can't stand my yearly examinations today.   But then, when there were such superstitions about women's bodies and unkind attitudes toward their reproductive systems. I can't imagine what she went through."

"And the archaic medical examinations she endured must have left her humiliated and without modesty and dignity," Emily added.

All three women sat silently then Aninki broke the silence.

"I remember a sermon on that passage the day after I heard Daniel was going to jail and Lo'laini was going to foster care. I felt so helpless. My head throbbed, so I turned on a Christian radio station in hopes that it would help me think. A woman minister explained how the culture ostracized women for long-term feminine bleeding. Those women were unclean, and as unclean, they kept out of sight. They were isolated from the community and forbidden from embracing their husbands or children. The community systematically shamed them."

"Shame again. Sometimes, no matter what women do, history shames them," Sandra sighed.

Aninki squeezed Sandra's hand again. "Imagine this woman in a crowd where people normally had nothing to do with her. Jesus called her out. He gave her a voice so he could tell the whole world he healed her and publicly commend her for her faith."

"Jesus took the shame away. He shamed the crowd," Emily smiled. "He healed her from the wrongfully placed shame as well as from the bleeding."

"I couldn't pray with you because I'm frightened of being disappointed again." Sandra started to tear up. "I prayed for Dad to stop drinking, Mom's death was too sudden to pray about, but at Mom's funeral, I prayed for Danny. That was the first time I saw Lo'laini. She was a little pink thing sleeping in her mother's arms. As I looked at his family—Danny, Mai and Lo'laini—I thanked God that Daniel wasn't using drugs anymore. But as time wore on, I could see at family gatherings that I was wrong. His intoxication was obvious. Watching addiction overtake Danny was like losing Dad all over again."

"I remember those days." Aninki got up to stretch. "No task in my life has been more difficult than watching cancer slowly eat away my daughter's body and health. I worried about

Lo'laini when I saw the addiction consuming Daniel's life. I prayed, and I tried to get Lo'laini out of his house, but that little girl loved her dad and wouldn't hear anything negative about him. I invited her over as much as I could. I even cleaned out my office to create a room for her, but he moved her to California, and I couldn't follow. In the end, there was nothing I could do but pray."

"Don't you see why I cannot pray?" asked Sandra, wiping her eyes again. "If I don't pray and she is not healed, I don't have to deal with the anger of an unanswered prayer, but if she's healed, I still have the option to join with everyone in praising God."

"Very businesslike and logical," Emily said, removing her hand from Sandra's. "That's quite a way to protect yourself. By refusing to pray, you free yourself from struggling with the Divine."

"No, Emily. I'm protecting my faith the only way I know how."

"But you'll still struggle with grief when someone you love is torn away from you, whether you pray or not. I know that lesson all too well." Aninki looked Sandra straight in the eye. "But it has been in my struggle with the Divine that I've found God's comfort. Greif is a consequence of living and loving, not of trusting God. When you love someone, you risk the pain that comes from losing them. In the end, we're all mortal, so loss is inevitable. My heart broke two times, over the loss of my husband and daughter, and it will break again if Lo'laini is taken from us." She returned to the pew to sit next to Sandra. "She's all I have left of my daughter."

"She's all I have left of my brother." Emily joined Aninki's tears.

"But Lo'laini is neither Mai nor Daniel. She is her own powerful and beautiful self. Losing her, if God allows Covid to take her away, will be a great grief. But it has been in the deepest moments of prayer when my petitions have grown from, *please God* to *why God* to *not my will but thine be done* that I have felt his greatest comfort and peace."

"That prayer sounds like defeatism to me." Sandra wiped her face, pushing away the tears.

"Not praying is defeatism. Leaving things to chance is fatalism, and there is little comfort in fatalism." Aninki's softened.

"When we were planning Daniel's funeral, you said faith kept slipping through your fingers. From what you've told us today, it seems like a lot of things that were dear to you have slipped from your grasp. You tried to hang on to your father, mother, your brother and now, Lo'laini. But you never had the power to hang on to any of these people. Whether you like it or not, people never belong to you. They belong to God. Even your faith doesn't belong to you. It was given to you by the grace of Christ. Just as you could not protect your loved ones, you cannot protect your faith. Maybe it's time you stopped trying to hang on to God and let him hang on to you. That's how I get the power to pray. Not my will but thine be done. It's my way of letting go and letting God hang on to me in the middle of my grief."

"My doubts are too great to pray that prayer."

"Oh, I have doubts too." Aninki smiled at Sandra, "Doubts lurk in my soul, and I battle with them every day. The prayer I use in my grief and doubt comes from the scripture from Mark nine twenty-four. 'Lord, I believe, help my unbelief.' But please hear me. If I've learned one thing in my fifty-one years, it's that there is no peace in trying to hold everything together by yourself. There's great serenity in letting go and praying for God's will."

"That's quite a sermon Aninki," Sandra said. "Sure, you didn't choose the wrong profession?"

"I have been thinking a lot about that lately," Aninki smiled.

"Sandra, you've already said the first part of that prayer three times today," Emily smiled.

"First part?" Sandra wrinkled her forehead. "You mean when I said I still believe? Yes, I did, but why is the second half so hard for me to say aloud?" She looked at the tapestries across the room from her: the field worker looking over Jesus's shoulder, the nanny demanding to be heard, the scullery maid reaching up to touch Christ's garment, and the haggard cook looking at Mary sitting at Jesus's feet.

Her eyes widened as she looked at the cross in front of the chapel. "It wasn't my faith that slipped through my fingers. You were always there, Lord. Even when I tried to push you away, you were always there. It was the people I loved who slipped through my grasp, and I was angry. I only hung on to them because I knew they couldn't hang on for themselves. And I loved them. I loved them so much. I tried so hard to keep everything together, but it fell apart anyway because they were never mine, to begin with. I was angry, Lord. Angry at you because you didn't strengthen my grasp so I could stop them from falling through and destroying themselves on the rocks of addiction and all that mess."

Sandra sighed, "But they were not mine. They belonged to you and to themselves. They belonged to you and themselves in all their fickleness, curiosity, grandeur, and beauty. The decisions they made were between you and them. I couldn't change them as hard as I tried. All those years trying to prop up Dad and Danny were exhausting. All the years of trying to hang on to everyone I love with a tight grip have exhausted me. I can't make things happen or change patterns that I did not establish, but I still love them, so help me give this burden to you. Please protect and care for the people I love but cannot control. It's not a matter of me giving them to you. It's a matter of me realizing they were never mine, to begin with."

Emily put her hand on Sandra's shoulder. "I remembered you writing a check to pay the phone and gas bills after Dad died."

"How old were you when you started to manage your family's finances?" Aninki asked.

"She was fourteen," Emily said.

"Actually, we had lawyers who took care of those things." Sandra waved her hand.

"But you made the family get the lawyers, Sandi. I remember when bill collectors started to call, and we almost lost everything. You called our uncles and made them call a board meeting to protect the estate from our father's negligence. From that day on, you were always the one who doubled checked our balances and made sure an adult knew when we were in the red."

"I prayed in those days. I prayed every night that God would stop Dad from drinking. But I guess Dad had some say in that decision as well."

"As you said, they not only belonged to God, but they also belonged to themselves," Aninki whispered, turning her eyes toward heaven. "And Lord, so does our Lo'laini. She is no longer small, and we cannot whisk her into our arms to protect her from all dangers. We open our arms to you, asking you to hold her because we cannot."

"Jesus, please don't let this illness take Lo'laini from us, but not my will," Sandra's voice cracked. "But thine be done. Lord, I do believe. Please help…" her voice became a whisper. "My unbelief."

"Amen," whispered Emily and Aninki.

†

Chapter Nineteen

Lo'laini's Rest: Discovering Home

<From: Lunigirl> <To: Karriebear>

Hey Karrie,

I am still not strong enough to sit up for a Zoom meeting, but I wanted to catch up so email will have to do. I am dictating to Aunt Emily 'because I can't sit up."

I'm finally home again. Aunt Emily told me you kept emailing her while I was in the hospital. She said you even called once. She set up a Zoom meeting to update you on how I'm doing, but sitting up is still really hard for me.

As you can tell, I made it through Covid, but it was iffy at times. They didn't know if I was going to get out of the hospital. I never want to be that sick again. I was aching with every breath, and I wasn't sure if I was ever going to breathe easily again. I do now, and I'm thankful for every breath I can take. Girl, wear the mask, social distance, and stay well. I don't want you to go through what I did.

Did I tell you how everyone realized I was sick? I ran out of the house after an argument with my aunts. I got lost. Then I thought I saw Mom and Dad alive again, I found out later it was really Aunt Emily and Tutu, and they led me back to the house. Weird, huh?

The whole time I was in the hospital, I felt like I was in some kind of in between world. I couldn't see or hear anything very well. I wasn't awake or asleep, and I was always gasping for air. Occasionally, a nurse would look in my eyes and smile. I was so grateful for those smiles because Tutu, Aunt Sandra, and Aunt Emily couldn't visit me.

I'm home now and glad of it. I'm still weak and have a lot of headaches, but overall, I'm doing okay. I don't have any problems breathing anymore. What I like most is feeling at home after all these years.

I've got to say that Aunt Emily, Aunt Sandra, and Tutu have gone through some sort of transformation. They act like they really like each other. They're cooking and laughing in the kitchen all the time.

Michael, the Jamaican cook from the estate's tea shop, became part of our bubble during our isolation. He and Aunt Sandra had this romantic thing, but she put it on hold. Well, it's not on hold anymore. It's great to see her so happy, and I love having him around. He's a great chef, and I think I'd like to study under him when I'm stronger.

Aunt Sandra now reads her Bible every day, and Aunt Emily attends a codependency meeting online. In addition, Aunt Emily reads a lot of recovery books. She reads them aloud to everybody, whether we want to hear them or not.

We go to the chapel together every Friday to pray together because Tutu says that's where Aunt Sandra finally let go of everything she was trying to manage on her own and gave it to Jesus. It's so odd to hear her pray aloud. She says she's prayed before, but I've never heard her. Sometimes we sing. That's my favorite part. We watch church services on YouTube and talk about the sermons afterward. Of course, not everyone agrees, but no one gets angry anymore over the things we disagree about. I can also talk about Dad without there being a major explosion. All my life, there was a simmering anger in the background at family reunions, and it's not here anymore. It may come back again, but it's gone for now, and as Aunt Emily always says, one day at a time.

Aunt Sandra and Tutu sat down with me the day after I came home from the hospital to make a schedule for my visits to Hawaii when I'm strong enough. I was dreading talking to Aunt Sandra about it, she and Tutu had it all planned out. I didn't have to worry about anything.

Tutu will be leaving at the end of the week for Hawaii. She's not sure if she'll keep the shop open. I always knew the shop wasn't her favorite thing. She kept it open at first to support grandpa and then to support Mama during cancer, but I never thought she would close it. She talked about going into the ministry, which isn't too much of a surprise because I know she studied theology, but I'm still in shock. Can't wait to see what will happen next in her life.

What's this I hear about you going to seminary? I always knew you were smart enough to go to graduate school, but I thought you didn't believe women should be in the pulpit. You're going to have to catch me up on that subject. When I talked with Aunt Sandra and Tutu about my visits to Hawaii, they said they might arrange for a layover in California for a couple of days so we could catch up.

I also heard you were living in Isabella's backyard. Good move!! I never thought you were safe at your mother's house. Sorry if it hurts you to hear me say that, but there it is. Your mom never seemed to fully grow up, and your safety was never her priority. (Okay, you can send me an angry email response if I shouldn't have said that.)

Sorry about Tom. (Aunt Emily told me. I guess you two had a great talk while I was sick.) I know in high school; I sometimes badmouthed him when I shouldn't have. You know my weird sense of humor. The truth is I thought he was a nice guy, and he really did seem to like you, but paper-thin people can give you awful paper cuts and they tear too easily. (Again, looking forward to your angry email about me mouthing off about this.)

Seriously, Karrie, I think Tom would have held you back. I know you're going to accomplish great things because I only love great people!!! When thinking about everything we've gone through, I think there was a light with us—a light greater and bigger than all the darkness around us.

I still miss Mom and Dad, but I'm glad for what I have in you, Tutu, and my aunts.

Let's Zoom next week. I can't make it too long without my bestie, who has always had my back,

Love ya,

Lo'laini,

(I forgot to tell you that I found out Josh is going to Oxford next year! So he's moving out here. What's up with that?)

✝

Chapter Twenty

A Perfect Home for a Portrait

Isabella's Tribute

"You know exactly why he's going out there," Karrie smiled and turned off her phone. "Clocking out!" she shouted from the kitchen as she headed out.

"Have a great day," Cindy said as Karrie punched out.

"It's so weird to see this place empty while doing business." Karrie looked into the empty dining area. "Serving takeout is a lot lonelier than having customers dine in."

Cindy punched in. "I never thought I'd say it, but I miss our cranky entitled customers."

"Agreed," Karrie laughed. "How weird is that? The good thing is that because there are no customers, I can go through the front door on my way out."

Cindy laughed, and Karrie walked through the dining area toward the reception area. Isabella stood somberly before the wall of portraits of her mentors. Five years earlier, Isabella introduced Karrie to the pictures on that wall and their histories after Karrie had a meltdown at work the night, she served some customers who spoke cruelly survivors of abuse in her presence.

Her mind drifted back to that significant conversation.

"Do you know who these people are?" Isabell asked Karrie as she pointed to the wall.

"No, I've never noticed them before. In the past, I only noticed—"

"You only noticed sombreros, maracas, guitarróns, and the lace mantilla. We also have pictures between them. People see what they want to see. I wish people would notice these pictures more often. The woman in the far corner is Maria Moreno. She worked for fair pay for agricultural workers and later became a Pentecostal minister. The woman above her is Rigoberto Menchu, and she's from Chimel, Guatemala. She's a peace activist, and she was awarded the Nobel Peace Prize in 1992 for her work in South America. The man in the upper right corner is Luis Palau. He's an evangelist in South America. Some people say he preached to greater crowds than Billy Graham. The center picture is of Gabriel García Márquez. He won the 1982 Nobel Prize for literature, and his works have been translated into dozens of languages. The man in the left corner is Edwin Bustillos. He was an agricultural engineer from the Sierra Madre in Mexico. He worked tirelessly to conserve desert plant life and to destroy the Mexican drug cartel."

Karrie fixed her eyes on the picture of Maria Moreno. Her broad smile and warm presence drew Karrie in.

"Do you know why your dessert was served at this restaurant?" Isabella asked. "I'm sorry to say it wasn't your cooking ability." She laughed and put her arm around Karrie. "It was the proposal you wrote. You have a way with words. Your descriptions caught both Alejandro's and my eyes. You have a way with words, Karrie."

Isabella looked at the restaurant wall. "Do you know what these people have in common besides passion and talent? They've all been criticized and misunderstood. I believe God gives passion and talent. The world gives unfair criticism. But God wins when we allow his passion and talent to override the world's criticism. I have this wall to express my passion, and I have a kitchen to express my talent. You have a voice. You've got to start using it."

Now Karrie reverently watched Isabella gazing at the same wall that had given Karrie such courage five years ago. Isabella seemed to be trembling and she wasn't sure if she should approach her. Karrie walked quietly behind Isabella and then she spoke.

"Five years ago, you told me what this wall meant to you. I'll never forget the lessons it taught me."

Isabella turned around and both women teared up. "God has given you a voice, Karrie. Have you found it yet?"

"I found many voices that have witnessed the same truth to me."

"Which truth?"

"Salvation. Redemption. Empowerment. Those are the recurring themes I guess." Karrie sat next to Isabella. "And all the roads that lead to me to love and Jesus."

"Not a bad message if you've got a passion to preach it."

Karrie put her arm around Isabella.

"Listen to the myriad of voices when you tell your story. They will remind you that you're not alone on this journey. There's not a dark tunnel you've struggled through, not a bitter tear, not a mountain that you've been forced to climb, that someone hasn't struggled with, cried about, or journeyed through before you. You're not alone. No one is alone on their faith journey."

Karrie leaned into Isabella's hug.

Isabella sighed, "I'm glad you're here. I'm adding a picture to my wall today." She held up a framed photograph of two farm workers dressed in a traditional Guatemalan clothing. "I found this picture while cleaning out my mother's things. I would like to introduce you to my mother, Agostina, and my father, Abisai. They had a hard life, but if my mother's diary was correct, it was a good life, and it was full of love. Their love gave birth to me. Where do you think I should put them?" Isabella asked, looking at Karrie.

"Why not beside Maria Moreno. She was the woman who caught my eye five years ago. I like her smile." Karrie answered. "Wasn't she the woman who worked with Caesar Chavez? Didn't she build a mission near the Arizona-Mexican border?"

Isabella smiled, "Yes, and it would have been about that time when Mom crossed the border. It's possible they could have met. Mom said in her diary that there was a mission on the Arizona border where she stopped on her way to California. It could have been Maria's mission."

Isabella hung a small hook next to the picture of Maria Moreno. The two pictures seemed natural together.

"That looks good," she said, wiping away a tear. "Maria Moreno was one of those people who made safe places for people in this dangerous world."

"Like someone else I know." Karrie moved closer to Isabella. "The world is a better place because of those people who make us feel safe by their mere existence. They overcame so we could know that we can overcome."

"It's a nice thought that this powerful woman might have comforted my mom." Isabella sat down to gaze at the portraits.

"I guess that's how it works. Our lives and struggles come together to weave the tapestry of faith that drives Christianity forward. We gain strength in our faith by witnessing each other's struggles, which helps us complete our journey."

"And find our homes." Karrie leaned her head on Isabella's shoulder.

Praise be to the God and Father of our Lord Jesus Christ, the Father of compassion and the God of all comfort, who comforts us in all our troubles so that we can comfort those in any trouble with the comfort we ourselves receive from God. For just as we share abundantly in the sufferings of Christ, so also our comfort abounds through Christ.

– 2 Corinthians 1:3–5

About the Author

Reverend Cheryl Kincaid studied Marriage and Family Therapy and has Master of Divinity.

She is the author of four books, Hearing the Gospel through Charles Dickens a Christmas Carol, The Little Clay Pot, The Little Candle That Was Frightened of the Dark and Karrie's Thorn, which is the prequel to A Forgotten Door Called Home.

Rev. Kincaid seeks to tell the story of God's comforting redemptive grace during an imperfect world. Rev. Kincaid confesses that many of her stories were inspired from witnessing God's redemptive grace unfold in wounded Christian's lives, including her own. Learn more about Pastor Cheryl at:

revcherylkincaid.com

dickensandchristianity.com

www.ingramcontent.com/pod-product-compliance
Lightning Source LLC
Chambersburg PA
CBHW052014190726
48295CB00012BA/308